THE
Original
1982

THE
Original
1982

LORI CARSON

WM
WILLIAM MORROW
An Imprint of HarperCollins*Publishers*

P

Car

5/3/13

This book is a work of fiction. The characters, incidents, and dialogue are drawn from the author's imagination and are not to be construed as real. Any resemblance to actual events or persons, living or dead, is entirely coincidental.

HarperCollins books may be purchased for educational, business, or sales promotional use. For information please write: Special Markets Department, HarperCollins Publishers, 10 East 53rd Street, New York, NY 10022.

FIRST EDITION

Designed by Diahann Sturge

Library of Congress Cataloging-in-Publication Data has been applied for.

ISBN 978-0-06-224529-8

13 14 15 16 17   OV/RRD   10 9 8 7 6 5 4 3 2 1

What matters in life is not what happens to you but what you remember and how you remember it.
—Gabriel García Márquez

THE
Original
1982

You were the first, Little Fish.

We were walking on Columbus Avenue from the Sheridan, the building where your father lived, to the Café Miriam, where I worked as a waitress. I had terrible morning sickness and had to sit on the curb to keep from throwing up. Your father told me to put my head between my knees.

The Café Miriam was a restaurant on the west side of Columbus. It was across the street from the Museum of Natural History and a big neighborhood hangout in those days. It was there your father and I first met. I was working brunches and lunches, mostly. I'd never waited tables before, but there wasn't much to it, just hard work.

I remember exactly where he was seated, at a four-top by the window, across from the bar. He had three friends with him. One was the music journalist Roberto Rodriguez, and the other two were fans or yes-men. Your father was famous, they said, the Bob Dylan of his country. When he saw me he grabbed his heart and gasped, pretending I was too beautiful to bear. He was a master at seduction, charming and bright with intelligent dark eyes and a Cupid's-bow mouth.

He could have any woman he wanted, and he had plenty. I was twenty-one, a former art school student and Long Island girl, slender with long dirty-blond hair and hazel eyes, pretty in a natural way. I still am, and it's thirty years later. Your father rightly predicted I'd be a handsome woman as I aged. He was thirteen years my senior, but looked even older than that. His hairline was receding and he wore a Hawaiian shirt with a pair of baggy jeans belted up high. He seemed more mature for other reasons, too. He was street-smart and well educated, the scrappiest dog on the block. He liked to win and was used to winning.

If you had inherited the best traits of both of us, you'd have been smart and a beauty, a lover of music, a sensitive girl. I'm fairly certain your father would have broken your heart the way he broke mine. He didn't want you to be born and never had any children after. He was his own child, the apple of his own eye: an artist, showman, and politician. I spared you that at least. But I spared you life itself and for that I'm filled with regret.

If I could go back to any day in my life, I'd go back to that morning on Columbus Avenue, morning sickness, head between my knees. I'd go back with courage. I'd say:

"Maestro, I'm not having an abortion. Get ready. You're going to have a child."

And since I'm the writer of this story, and can do whatever I want, that's what I'll do. Go back to that day in 1982.

Part 1

One

Gabriel Luna has a *Daily News* rolled up in his back pocket. He's looking forward to his breakfast, eggs over easy with bacon and sausage both, maybe a side of ham. He doesn't much like having to deal with anyone else's problems. Not even mine, and he loves me. That's what he says and what all his friends and former girlfriends tell me. But I'm pregnant and he doesn't want me to be pregnant. He can't forget about it either, although I try not to mention it. But I'm sick, I'm sick as hell all the time.

I love him with another kind of sickness. The kind that makes me forget I have an opinion of my own or any wishes that don't fall in neatly with his. I'm young but this doesn't quite explain it. There's a wound in me that I know about but have not yet begun to examine and take apart. It makes me compliant, and more than that: it makes me believe I have no right to my own life.

Gabriel and I make love every night except for the ones we spend apart. We use no birth control other than his pulling out at the last second. Every once in a while, he doesn't pull out. It's a special gift he gives me.

"This is for you, Mami. Nobody else."

He says it in a rush as he comes. Coming inside me is what distinguishes the sex he has with me from the sex he has with other women, all unprotected. He gives me a venereal disease that year, too, a gift that keeps on giving.

But this isn't a story about Gabriel Luna or his selfishness. This is a story about a girl who gets to be born. One of those nights, when he doesn't pull out, it happens. Your life begins.

In 1982, there aren't any protesters yet, no right-to-lifers. People are still reeling from illegal abortion, still euphoric about the fact that there is choice. Even the word *abortion* has no stigma. It means freedom, liberation, the right to choose.

Not that I'm aware of all that.

I believe you are a speck of protoplasm and that I'll have other chances.

I think there's no way he will allow it.

I watch Gabriel eat his breakfast at the Café Miriam. It makes me sick to smell the cooked meat. I want to rest my head on the table as he reads aloud to me from the paper. He explains what is really going on in the world. I love listening to him. I love his accent, the way when he speaks English he stresses the wrong syllables and confuses his prepositions. He reads between the lines to see America's complicity in all the world's problems. He calls the U.S. North America out of respect for his own country and all the countries of Latin America. He feels superior to the North Americans, who are soft and ignorant, but feels better than his own people, too, because they don't live at the center of things, in New York City, as he does. His intention is to show these *norteamericanos* what he can do. Then go home a hero.

We sip our coffee at the Café Miriam. We don't even mention you at that breakfast. I'm thinking about the abortion, though. I'm worried it will hurt. I remember a girl I knew at school. Her name was Melanie Parker. What comes to mind is that she never spoke to her boyfriend again after her abortion. She told me she couldn't even stand to look at his face.

Two

The next day we go to the clinic. It's in a hospital on the Upper East Side. Gabriel is afraid he'll be recognized but he comes anyway. He's wearing aviator sunglasses with dark lenses and a Mets baseball cap, pulled down low. If anyone sees him he'll say he's here with a friend. He's a Catholic, too. It's not okay with him. But it's more okay than the alternatives.

I leave him sitting in the waiting room and go with the nurse to change into a blue hospital gown, open in the back. I lie down on a cold metal table, legs spread apart, my icy feet resting on the metal stirrups. I'm given something to relax me and start to give in to it.

Just as I'm about to go under, it hits me. I can't go through with it.

I open my eyes and try to sit up.

"Wait."

"It's okay," the nurse says. She's holding my hand. She's only a few years older than I am.

"Lie back now," says the doctor.

But it's not okay and I won't lie back, though my limbs are heavy from the sedation. I feel as if I'm levitating off the table, climbing legless to the floor. The room is tilting left and right but I make it to the wall and move toward the door. I'm aware of a commotion behind me as I close my eyes and fall to my knees.

"I want to keep the baby," I tell them.

Another nurse, or maybe she's an aide, makes her way to me through the confusion. She takes hold of my arm and helps me up, leads me back to the rows of beds where the women who have had abortions are recovering. I get into a bed to sleep off the drugs, pull a thin blanket over my back. When I wake up a little while later, I remember. I haven't gone through with it. I'm still pregnant! I'm flooded with relief.

Gabriel is so mad, he won't talk to me. He takes me back to my small apartment on East Seventy-eighth Street and leaves me at the door. I climb up the ladder into my loft bed and sleep for twenty-four hours. When I wake up, I'm hungry for mint chip ice cream. The cats wind around my ankles. They're hungry, too. I fill their bowl from a bag of store-brand cat food. I open the half refrigerator stuck in the hallway near the bathroom. It's empty except for some wilted celery and a couple of packets of soy sauce. A rotten smell emanates from it and turns my stomach. For a moment I'm terrified. How will I take care of a baby when I can barely look after these two cats and myself?

Three

A few days later, Gabriel leaves for Puerto Rico to play some concerts. He'll be gone three weeks. In the original 1982, I go with him. I wear a purple bikini. I'm flat-chested, skinny as a boy. He tells me all the women on the beach wish they had a body like mine and I feel proud. We've put the abortion in the back of our minds or maybe we're pretending the pregnancy never happened.

Every afternoon we walk from the beach through the hotel lobby to have lunch in the restaurant. A guy plays the piano there all day.

"Baby, how come he plays in the lobby of a hotel and you play in a stadium?" I ask.

Gabriel laughs, but I'm sincere. I'm trying to figure out what makes someone succeed or fail. I want to be successful like him. I write songs. I play the guitar a little. I think if he can do it, so can I.

In his band, there are two girl singers, Estelle and Mildred. Mildred is down-to-earth, a Puerto Rican American woman who writes the vocal arrangements and gets along with everybody. I ask her questions about how she got started. I sing one of my songs to her on the beach.

"One day, maybe I'll sing with your band," she says encouragingly.

The other one, Estelle, is harder to read. A Jewish girl sort of passing for Latina, she's a six-footer with wide hips and big legs. I can tell Gabriel likes her. Two weeks into that trip I find out he's going to her hotel room after rehearsal.

But none of that matters. Because this time I don't go with him to Puerto Rico. I stay behind in New York to work extra shifts at the restaurant. I stop drinking alcohol and start saving my money.

Four

At the Café Miriam my fellow waitresses are artists, dancers, and musicians. We're proud to be nonprofessionals. We're only waiting tables until our circumstances change.

The customers know it. They ask us what we *really* do. They smile and say, "Someday I'll say I knew you when."

We believe it's true. It's just a matter of time.

Sofia is in an off-off-Broadway play. Janelle is a member of a modern dance company. Nina makes sculpture out of things she finds on the street.

Vicky, our manager, tries to bring us back down to earth. "Quit your daydreaming and clear table six," she says lightly. She's pretty cool as far as managers go. She has long red hair and the whitest skin covered in freckles.

I'm not the only one at the restaurant who's pregnant. Another girl, Callie, is, too. She and her boyfriend are getting married in a couple of weeks. She's an actress but says she'll take a break from auditioning once her baby is born. She looks as tired as I feel. I catch her eye and we smile.

When I leave the restaurant at the end of my shift, it's still light out. Every day it gets dark a little later. Excitement rides high in my chest. It's almost spring in New York, and the scent of it is in the air, floating down from the tight buds of apple blossom trees.

I talk to you all the time, Little Fish. I tell you everything I see: Look at all the people walking with a lighter step, winter coats over their arms, ready for warmer days.

Five

In 1982, the most popular names for girls are Jessica, Jennifer, and Ashley. But I'm not one to follow convention. My own name, Lisa, was so common growing up, it was usually paired with my last initial. I want yours to be yours alone. I consider the names of flowers and birds. I think of family names:

Pearl, Rose, Lily, Sparrow. I change my mind every day. I like boys' names for girls, too—Jamie, Syd, Max—and the names of colors, Blue or Green like the songs by Joni Mitchell.

I play you lullabies on my Martin. Before you, the songs I wrote were lonely songs, but now I write love songs to you and your father.

Gabriel gets back from Puerto Rico and calls from the airport.

"Hey, I miss you," he says tenderly. "Meet me at the house."

Although I'm dead tired, I shave my legs, get in a taxi, and ride across the park. I let myself into his apartment and get into bed to wait for him. When I hear his key in the lock, my heart starts to beat crazily. His footsteps on the hardwood floor, the sound of his voice as he says my name, his passionate kiss, his skin on my skin. Loving him is a drug I need to live.

In the original 1982, it's unbelievable what happens. I get pregnant again and have another abortion. Gabriel breaks up with me. He says he's come to the realization that I don't give him anything. I write him a poem about the irony of that statement. I've given him two little babies and he's helped me flush them down the drain. We're apart for two weeks, then he calls and we get back together.

But there can be no second pregnancy, not while I've got you in my belly. I've made my decision and there's no changing it. Gabriel tries every way he knows to get me to reconsider. He argues, he reasons. He's sugar one day and vinegar the next. He brings me ice cream and spreads Vic's VapoRub on my chest when I catch a cold. He calls me Pajarito, an endearment that means "little bird."

Then he punishes me and doesn't call. He's seeing Estelle, I'm sure of it, and others, too. He's never been faithful, but he doesn't try so hard to hide it now.

I think of you growing inside me and it gives me the will to stand up to him. I think of your tiny heart forming, your webbed hands and feet. I go to the library and take out books called *Your Baby* and *What to Expect When You're Expecting*. I find out it's normal to run up the stairs and feel out of breath, or gag on the subway at the smell of someone's dirty hair.

I worry a lot. Every time I feel a little ache or pinch, I'm afraid something will go wrong. I worry about what it will be like once you're born. How will I know how to take care of you? But then I see all the babies and children in strollers and playgrounds, on every street in New York City, and think about how they all got here the same way. Some of those children were born to mothers who were as scared and baffled as me. I think maybe it will be okay. Maybe it's even good that I'm young. I'll be able to chase after you and keep up with you. There's nothing I won't do to make sure you have a happy life. Isn't that a law of physics, when you change one thing, all the others change, too? Maybe even Gabriel Luna will be transformed.

Six

Gabriel plays at the Vantage on Tuesday nights. These are special Latin-meets-jazz concerts. He's always nervous no one will show up, but every week there's a line around the block. It's thrilling to go with him. I get dressed up and hold his hand as we run alongside all the people waiting to get in. Sitting in the audience among the crowd of salsa fans, I marvel at his talent, his ability to capture the crowd. When he morphs one of his own songs into Marvin Gaye's "Sexual Healing," the women in the audience start to howl, and jealousy comes over me like a creeping rash.

Backstage Eddie nods hello. He's the bandleader, a trumpet player and well-respected *patrón* in Latin music circles. Carole-Ann, his beautiful blond wife, leans up against the wall beside him. She's all right, but because she's a wife and I'm a girlfriend, she's never as friendly to me as she is to the wives of the other musicians. Or maybe it's because things are tense between Eddie and Gabriel lately. Eddie thinks Gabriel should be satisfied with things as they are instead of always trying to overshadow him. He wants Gabriel to keep singing in his band, keep making hit records. He doesn't understand why Gabriel wants to woo a white audience who will never truly appreciate lyrics written in Spanish and rhythms they can't feel in their bones.

But Gabriel is a star. Anyone can see he's going places and won't be taking any of us with him. Not even me.

Carole-Ann waves me over. She's wearing a sparkly dress, snug against her curves. She offers me a cigarette from her silver case, but I turn it down. Sometimes I smoke with her even though I don't smoke. "You sure?" she asks, and I come close to telling her that I'm pregnant. But who knows what she'd do with the information? She lights one for herself and blows the smoke to the side, away from me. "You coming to Europe?" she asks. I've heard that there are some dates coming up—Brussels and Amsterdam and Paris, but I haven't been invited.

"I don't think so," I say. "I probably have to work."

"Gabriel has your plane tickets," she says.

But Gabriel hasn't said anything to me about that.

I watch him from across the room. He's talking, moving his

hands, his fans listening in rapt attention. Always there are women, beautiful and young, or older and accomplished. I'm on the lookout for the ones who are his type. Gabriel says I always pick the wrong ones, that he's not even attracted to the women I fear. But of course it's the cheating itself that makes me afraid. When I see a pretty girl approach him, my heart sinks. Maybe she'll be the one he takes to Europe.

Seven

At the women's clinic in the Flatiron District, I wait with a half dozen other girls in the reception area. We read magazines or watch the small TV monitor. We look up whenever the receptionist opens her window to call out a name. "The doctor will see you now," she says.

Dr. Nancy isn't really a doctor. She's a nurse practitioner. A lot of girls I know go to see her for exams and birth control. She's very tall and confident, a little intimidating. Holistic before holistic becomes fashionable.

When it's my turn, I go through the door and down the hallway, into the examining room.

"Hello there," Dr. Nancy says breezily as she comes in a few minutes later with my folder in her hands. "What can I do for you today?" She doesn't seem shocked when I tell her my news. "Congratulations," she says, not unkindly.

Dr. Nancy examines me and takes some blood. She says everything looks good. She tells me what vitamins I should be taking and how important it is to eat the right foods. She says she won't actually be delivering my baby. Her partner at the

clinic, Dr. Diamond, has an affiliation with a hospital, and
he'll be the one.

"I assume you have health insurance?" Dr. Nancy asks. I
tell her that I don't and show her the pocketful of cash I've
brought, tips from weeks of waitressing. "Come with me," she
says, and walks me across the hall to sit down with her office
manager for guidance.

Turns out I need health insurance, of course, but there's no
way I can afford it. I figure I have two options. I can go to Gabriel and ask him to pay for it or I can ask my parents. I'm not
confident either will help me. I'm estranged from my mother
and father and haven't spoken to them in months. If they do
help, I know it will come with all kinds of strings attached.

Yet I can't bring myself to ask Gabriel. I can already see the
furious look in his eye, the stern set of his jaw.

So I take the train out to Long Island to the house where I
grew up. My parents live in a modest house in a middle-class
neighborhood on the south shore of Long Island. It's a split-
level surrounded by neighbors and big trees. I've turned down
my mother's offer for a ride from the station, told her I wanted
to walk instead. I'm putting off the moment when I'll have to
see them. I haven't been back in more than a year.

As I approach the house, I'm nervous. I can see my mother
waiting to greet me at the front door. She's shorter than I
am and a little more sturdy. She teaches reading to grammar
school kids. Blond and blue-eyed, girl-next-door pretty, she
has deep dimples when she smiles, which she's doing now.

My mother holds the screen door open, hugs and kisses me
until I pull away. It's been a long time. Our last argument is
nearly forgotten.

The house is frozen in the early 1970s: dark paneling,
orange-gold carpet. There's a wallpaper mural in the dining

room of a street scene in Paris. It's looked like this for as long as I can remember. My father is nowhere to be seen.

My mother asks me if I'm hungry, and we settle in the kitchen. Me at the Formica table in the chair that was mine, she at the stove. She makes cheese and eggs for me, the way she always has. I'm not sure if my stomach will stand for it today, but it's comforting anyway. Through the window screen behind her, I see the familiar treetops and telephone lines.

"Where's Dad?" I ask.

"Oh, he's around here somewhere," she says distractedly.

My father is a tall, handsome man with olive skin and hazel eyes. He's one of the smartest people I know, an engineer and inventor. He's got a strong moral code, too; never has more than a single cocktail, wouldn't in a million years cheat on my mother.

Still, he's a hard man to have as a father. He seems to think my artistic inclinations are a rebellion that can be cured with silence and a hard line. He looks at me as if I'm pretending not to be smart just to spite him.

I hear his footsteps overhead. He's probably in his room, or in the attic working on some gadget.

"Mom, I need to tell you something, and I don't want you to tell Daddy." She looks alarmed even before I say it. "I'm pregnant."

Her blue eyes are unblinking; still my excitement makes me hopeful.

"Are you sure?" she asks. "You've been to the doctor? What does Gabriel say?"

I shrug my shoulders. The gesture tells her that Gabriel is not on board, that I'm alone in this.

"What are you going to do?" she asks, and I feel a familiar disappointment.

"I'm going to have it," I say, excitement dashed. Her reaction is not what I want. I want her to reassure me, help me to feel everything will be okay. I want her to say that no matter what happens she and my father will be there for me. But she doesn't say any of that. We're quiet as she serves me breakfast.

"The thing is I need a little help," I say finally.

"What kind of help?" she asks, and I feel angry. What difference does it make what kind? What kind of question is that? But I swallow my anger because I need her to pay for the insurance. When I explain, she looks relieved.

"I'll call Blue Cross today and see if we can put you on our policy," she says. "If not, we'll figure something else out."

"Thank you," I say, *thanks a lot.*

We hear my father coming down the stairs and stop talking.

"Hi, Dad," I say. My father is forty-six years old, a little more gray than he was last year. He takes his place at the head of the table. I think his charisma comes from his confidence and the way he keeps himself aloof.

"Do you want coffee?" my mother asks him.

He ignores her. "Everything okay?" he asks me instead.

"Yes," I say. "Everything's fine." I know he'll find out about the pregnancy eventually, but it won't be from me.

"What's the latest?" he asks.

My mother pours his coffee and I tell him about the celebrities I've met at the restaurant. Dustin Hoffman. Bob Fosse. "Do you know who that is, Dad?" He does. They've been to see *A Chorus Line.* When I run out of things to say, I ask him about the Yankees, his favorite team. I can hear the clock ticking and the hum of the refrigerator in his silences. After a while he says it's good to see me and heads back up to his room.

My mother and I take our coffee outside to the deck overlooking the backyard with its tall trees, sloping green-brown lawn, and rusted swing set. I think about how I used to race my sister to be first down the slide after it snowed. The whole neighborhood was new then. There was a drive-in movie theater right over the fence. It got torn down when they built the expressway.

My mother asks me how I'm feeling and I tell her the morning sickness is pretty bad.

"I was sick my whole pregnancy with you," she says.

"I think it's supposed to pass in the second trimester," I tell her hopefully.

"It didn't with you," she says.

It figures, I think. Even in utero, we couldn't get along. But I don't say that.

Later, she gives me a ride back to the train. We embrace awkwardly across the front seat of the car.

"I'll call you tomorrow," she says, worry in her eyes. I get out quickly and run up the stairs to the platform. Waiting for the train, I see her Toyota make a slow crawl around the corner, as if she's too shaken to even step on the gas.

Eight

At the Café Miriam, I'm working double shifts. I go until I can't anymore, then fall into bed and pass out. Waiting tables with morning sickness is not so different from the days when I used to drag myself into work after a night out drinking. Just like then, I head straight to Will, Café Miriam's bartender, for his special hangover remedy and it helps to settle my stomach.

It's the double shifts that wear me out. My clothing takes on the odor of cooking grease. My hair always stinks of it. I start to resent the customers for every annoying thing they do. I stand at the coffee station and stare out the windows at the free people walking by.

One day Janelle comes in and says she's got some dirt. She says Lois, a dancer who worked at the restaurant for a short time, is giving sensual massages out of her apartment. "That means at the end of the massage? She gives the guy a hand job."

"I bet that's not all she's doing," Nina says. "Why stop there?"

We talk about what we'd do and what we'd never do. We've all thought about prostitution. Not about doing it, exactly, but about the fact that we could. It's an option for attractive young women and we know it. We also know the money is supposed to be really good.

"It's not that different from having sex with a guy after he takes you out to dinner," Nina says. "If the guys were decent, it wouldn't be so bad."

"But they wouldn't be decent. They'd be fat and old," Janelle says.

"Ewww," says Sofia. "They'd have hairy backs and bad breath."

"Well, if you could pick the ones you wanted, it wouldn't be so bad," Nina says.

A few days later, I'm coming out of a deli on Broadway and practically bump into Lois. She looks great, as always. She's a beautiful girl with a dancer's body. Her hair is pulled back. She's all cheekbones and long green eyes. Her gaze falls to my belly. You jut from my thin frame like a little melon.

"Am I seeing what I think I'm seeing?"

"Hey, Lois." All I can think about is professional hand jobs.

"Is the father the Mexican guy?"

"He's not Mexican, but yeah," I say. "Gabriel."

"He's a musician, right?"

"Uh-huh, a singer."

"You going to get married?"

"I don't think so." I'm dying to ask her about the sensual massage, but can't think of a way to do it.

"Well, he has to support you even if you don't get married," Lois says. "You know that, right?"

"Yeah, I guess." She doesn't know Gabriel. "I'll figure something out," I say.

"Don't be stupid." She digs into her bag and hands me a card. It has her picture on one side and her phone number on the other. "Here. It sounds like you need some practical advice. I know about this. My sister went through it. Call me."

She's a very practical girl, I'm thinking. She's probably never loved someone so much she couldn't eat or sleep. I can't imagine proposing such a thing to Gabriel. It would only make him angry. My plan is to wait him out. I think if I tread lightly enough, if I never ask him for anything, maybe he'll give me what I want.

"Call me," Lois says again.

She's a girl who knows how to take care of herself, whatever it takes. I put her card in my pocket.

Nine

By summer, the morning sickness is gone and I'm only ravenous. I'm hungry for everything, all the time. Potatoes, cake, bread, pizza, enchiladas with sour cream, spinach pie from

the Greek diner on Madison. I can eat all day and wake up
in the middle of the night starving. I've always been skinny
without trying, one of those enviable girls who can eat anything and never gain a pound, but I've never eaten like this
before. My belly gets rounder and bigger. I don't know how
much of it is you and how much the midnight pizza, the morning coffee cake. I could win a pie-eating contest. I could beat
the hot-dog-eating champ at Coney Island.

I look at my body in the mirror and am amazed to see I
actually look pregnant. *Your Baby* has color illustrations that
show sort of what you look like. If the pictures are accurate,
you resemble a little alien. I study the diagrams. They label
your shoulder, your eye, the chambers of your heart. You're
developing ears and your eyes are starting to open. The book
says you're the size of an orange.

My mother puts the word out to her friends, the ones who
have daughters with daughters, now three and four, and as the
weeks go by, I'm given a secondhand crib, a changing table,
and a stroller. The world loves a baby on the way. Maybe she's
told them that I'm doing it alone; the cardboard boxes of dona-
tions accumulate. They pile up in front of the marble fireplace
mantel in my small studio apartment. The cats use them for
scratching posts.

My mother calls nearly every day. She proposes schemes to
get Gabriel to marry me, but none of them make sense. She
doesn't know Gabriel and mistakes him for a normal man, one
who can be tricked or talked into doing something he doesn't
want to do. I know he's proud of the fact that he doesn't care
what anybody thinks, and only does exactly what he wants.
To me, he seems a different species from my family, and I like
that about him, because I've always felt like I'm a different
species, too.

Still, it's nice to have my mother with me. She likes to come into the city to see musicals on Broadway. I don't like them much but go with her anyway. The air-conditioning feels good and it's comforting to have her company. We go to museums on the Upper East Side. The Whitney is right by my apartment and is small enough to see in its entirety. We stand in front of a black painting by Mark Rothko and laugh.

"Even I could do that," my mother says.

My youthful rebellion has been cut short by your lovely form pushing against me, the way I once pushed against everything. I listen to my mother tell me I could run a day-care center, or get a degree in education and teach as she does. I try not to let it get to me, although often it does.

Every day I play my guitar. I always have a new song I'm working on. Every one is better than the one before. I try to write melodies that go to unexpected places. Gabriel loves that about my songs. When he shows me a new chord, I surprise him with a whole new batch. "Pajarito, you are the best female songwriter I know," he says. The songs make him fall in love with me again. That's what it feels like.

But not even my songs can make up for this thing that I am doing to him. He kisses me good-bye and disappears for a week. I take the phone to bed with me so I won't miss his call. When he resurfaces, he says, "Baby, where *are* you?" As if I've been the one avoiding him. "Come over," he says, and I do, but he doesn't want to talk about you.

By Christmastime you'll be here. It's hard to imagine Christmas in the heat of July. People will be walking quickly on the street, holding their coats closed against the wind. The air will have a crisp bite to it. Christmas tree vendors will travel from Maine and Vermont to set up on Broadway and fill the street with the scent of pine needles. I'll wrap you in a soft blanket and take you to see the shop windows at Macy's and Bergdorf Goodman, buy you woolen mittens and hats. Fat snowflakes will fall. We'll get a tree and decorate it with white lights.

I'll be a mother. And Gabriel will be a father, whether he likes it or not. I can't help but picture our tree set up in a corner of his living room, a fire burning in the fireplace, all together, a family.

Ten

I tell Gabriel I need to talk to him and we make a date to meet at his place at the Sheridan. The apartment is technically a two-bedroom, but Gabriel has knocked down a couple of walls, put in French doors, and turned the second bedroom into an office. Except for the fireplace, there's nothing cozy or charming about it. The walls are covered with framed photographs of him at different stages of his career and posters of his concerts from all over the world. The furniture is cheap and kind of tacky. Next to the king-size bed, a fancy lamp sits conspicuously on an end table, an obvious gift from another woman. There's absolutely no reason why any woman in her right mind would want to live there. Except I do. I want to move in and make the office into a baby's room. I want the three of us to live together as a family.

I take the bus across town in the early evening. The light casts a beautiful glow on the buildings of the Upper West Side. They look especially three-dimensional, like an Edward Hopper painting. The sky is a deep blue, strewn with a few cumulous clouds dipped in purple. It makes me glad to be alive just to witness it. The world is so beautiful, Little Fish.

I get off the bus at Columbus Avenue and it's just a few steps to the entrance of the Sheridan. I take a deep breath and enter the building, heart already pounding.

The doorman gives me a wave and I make my way to the elevator around the corner. My mouth is dry. I'm nervous I'll be shot down before I've even been invited inside.

Gabriel is waiting for me in the doorway. "Hi, baby." He embraces me.

I'm wearing a dress he thinks looks good on me. It's tight across the belly, but I've managed to close the zipper. My legs are bare and tan. I've got a little makeup on, but not too much. It takes a lot of thought to be the girl he wants me to be.

He leads me directly to the bedroom, although I attempt to resist. I'm hoping to speak to him while I've still got his attention, while he's full of desire and in a good mood. The changes to my body excite him. My normally small breasts are spilling out of my bra. I probably seem like a completely different woman to him.

"Wait, wait," I say as he unzips my dress. "Can we talk first?"

"Let's talk second," he says.

So we begin our talk after making love, sheets tangled around us.

"Baby, don't you want to see your daughter grow up?" I ask him. My heart is fluttering in my throat.

"I want to see *you* grow up," he says, and I hear the beginning of anger in his voice. "You can stay here whenever you want. Why would you want to *live* here? You love having your own place."

"But I want us to live together as a family," I say.

"*¡Puta su madre!* I'm sick of this shit!" He pulls the sheet back and gets out of bed.

"We're not a family," he says. "You're my girlfriend and you're doing this thing I don't want you to do. You're forcing this thing that I don't want. Do you hear me? It's not going to be good. I'm telling you right now." His voice escalates as he says this. By the last of it, he's shouting and I'm cowering under the covers. I don't know what to do when he gets mad. I go numb. I can't think at all.

Minutes later, I find him on the couch watching videos on MTV. He takes my hand and kisses it. "I'm sorry I lost my temper, baby. Do you want to order some Chinese food? Go grab a menu from the kitchen."

I get the menu from a kitchen drawer and come back, sit beside him on the couch. We decide what we want and I call in the order.

We watch a video by an Australian band called Men at Work. The song has a reggae feel. It's called "Down Under." I can see Gabriel's wheels turning. He's moving to the music, thinking about how he can do something like that. He's watching the lead singer and seeing himself there instead.

Eleven

Before I knew your father, I didn't know who or what I wanted to be. I'd dropped out of school and was estranged from my family. I drank too much, stayed out all night, smoked a joint if I had one with my morning coffee. I had a number of boyfriends, but nothing ever lasted very long. I'd leave them at the bar, or in their beds, and make my way home alone. I can't tell you how many times I lost my keys and had to climb through that front window on East Seventy-eighth Street, which wasn't easy. You had to balance on a wrought-iron banister and reach across to the window. Drunk as I was, it's a miracle I never fell and cracked my skull.

Once a burglar climbed in that window when I wasn't home. He didn't steal a thing from me, because there was nothing to steal. I had a TV with a wire hanger for an antenna. The thief made his way from my building into the house next door and robbed a rich guy who was very unhappy about it. I had to have a gate put on the window. After that, when I lost my keys, I was out of luck.

When I met Gabriel, he was like a father to me in some ways. I needed to be loved by a strong man. I needed guidance and care, someone to tell me what was what.

Every day that first year, I took the crosstown bus at Seventy-ninth Street and met him on the West Side. Total strangers couldn't help but smile when they saw how much in love we were. Walking around the neighborhood, arms wrapped around each other, the world went slightly out of focus around us.

Being in love with him gave me confidence. He thought I was smart and I felt smart. He thought I was talented and I knew it was true. We played each other songs on the guitar, read to one another from the books we loved, talked about everything and anything. Sometimes, when it rained, we went to the movies all day, from one theater to the next.

We traveled to faraway places, for his concerts, or for fun. I'd never been anywhere before. We played dominoes and rode

bicycles in a Greek seaport town; had breakfast in Paris in a
room with a view of the Seine; raced at dawn to a plane waiting on a Bogotá runway; listened to the waves crash, late at
night, on a beach in St. Barts.

I learned how to be a lover, how to please and be pleased. He
told me stories and asked me to make them up for him, too.
We spun each other's fantasies out of thin air.

Sometimes, in a perfect moment, I'd hold my breath to
make time stop. I'd make a deal with God or whoever it is that
listens to prayers in the dark. I'd say, "If I can hold my breath
for forty-five seconds, you'll let it stay just like this."

Gabriel didn't drink at first. He'd gone to AA. He said I
should watch my drinking, too, so I stopped. I still smoked
pot, though. I left a baggie of it under his mattress to smoke
when I couldn't sleep, which happened a lot when I waited for
him to come home after a gig and he was late. Gabriel found
the pot and freaked out. He said drugs were for lowlifes. So I
quit that, too. For the first time since I was fifteen, I had no
substances or alcohol in my body. My love for him was all the
drug I needed.

But after a while, for some reason, we started drinking
again and right away things took a turn for the worse, and our
magical connection began to erode. I think it was the three-
somes that did the most damage. Fantasies were one thing; it
didn't mean I could bear to see him do the things he did to
me to someone else.

Sometimes I found girls of my own in the bars on Columbus Avenue. I kissed them in bathroom stalls. It was easy to
become him when I was drunk enough. Once I even brought
one back to his bed when he was out of town.

"You seem like the kind of girl who knows what to do," that

girl said to me, though it wasn't true. I was accumulating se-
crets to beat him at his own game.

Things change. No matter how long you can hold your
breath.

Twelve

One day I get a call from my landlord. I've heard rumors from
my neighbors that he wants to sell our building, a charming
brownstone on Seventy-eighth Street between Fifth and Madison. The gossip is he wants to make it into a single-family
home, but he can't do it unless we agree to leave. The building
is rent-controlled, which means we can live in it forever with
only small increases in rent, an amount determined by the city
and not the landlord.

Some people have lived in my building for more than thirty
years, mostly single, older women. They worry about where
they'll go. I pay only three hundred a month for my place, a
tiny first-floor studio, and the ladies who have lived here for de-
cades probably pay half that. I feel sorry for them. They seem
fragile, brittle, with their home-dyed hair and pale skinny
legs, coming down the stairs in worn bathrobes. I can't imagine a worse fate than to grow old, alone in one room, and then
be asked to leave it. At twenty-four, it's impossible to imagine
becoming like them. Being an old woman is something I think
I'll escape somehow.

My landlord's office is in a run-down building in the West
Thirties near Penn Station. I take the number 6 train down
to Thirty-third Street and walk west. It's a beautiful summer

day. I love looking into all the shop windows, love the way the
city makes me feel private in public, part of a big world full of
people walking with purpose.

My landlord is a middle-aged man with thinning dark hair
and wire-frame glasses. He sits behind a large metal desk.
Without a greeting, he motions for me to take a seat, and I do.
I'm wearing a man's white shirt and black pants, top button
undone. I've tried to look presentable for our meeting. It's not
so obvious that I'm pregnant.

"So, Miss Nelson, you may have heard we have an interest in your apartment." He has an accent. I'm not sure from
where. Israel, maybe.

"The thing is I don't have any money to move," I tell him.
"And the rent is so low. I can't see how I could afford to live
somewhere else."

He's ready for my response. Seems to already have an
amount in mind, as do I.

"Miss Nelson, we're prepared to offer you five thousand dollars to vacate the apartment. This will greatly help with your
moving costs and other expenses."

Five thousand dollars is a lot of money in 1982. I can rent a
very decent place on the West Side for under a thousand.

"Well, I appreciate the offer," I say. "But I'm thinking about
what it's going to cost to pay the higher rent for a year. I don't
think I can do it for less than fifteen thousand."

My landlord sits quietly, plays with his ink blotter. I have
no idea what he's thinking. He sighs and rises from his chair.
Behind him is a big window looking out onto the buildings
across the alley. He turns to face it, and we both watch the
people in their offices, lit by fluorescent lights. Finally, he
turns back to me.

"I can tell you, Miss Nelson, it's probably not going to

happen, but I'll talk it over with my partners. Hopefully, we can come to a compromise."

I thank him and make my way back to the elevator, down to the street, and outside to the beautiful day.

That fifteen thousand will rent a place big enough for the two of us and the cats. That's what I'm thinking. I'm not going to take a penny less.

My landlord calls a week later and agrees to the fifteen thousand. I start looking for a bigger apartment, one with a garden.

Thirteen

For the ultrasound test, the technician covers my belly with a cool gel. I stare at the empty screen, watching anxiously, until magically you appear in the shape of a lima bean, or a seashell. I'm twenty weeks pregnant. The technician, a middle-aged Indian woman, is gentle and kind. She points to your head, to your foot, to your heart. She helps me to make sense of what I see. Then she freezes your fuzzy silhouette on the screen, takes a Polaroid of it, peels off the back, and hands me a picture of you to keep.

"Looks like you've got yourself a little girl," Dr. Nancy says. Although, of course, I've known that from the start. She lets me hear your heartbeat, for the first time, using a special kind of stethoscope. She listens first and counts, watching the clock. Then she places the earpiece in my ear.

"It's beating so fast!" I say, truly shocked.

"That's right," she says. "That's how we're sure it's your baby we're listening to and not you."

I catch the tears that fall with my tongue. I can't stop laughing. I think of that Joni Mitchell song about laughing and crying being the same release.

Dr. Nancy smiles. "Now you can start thinking about baby names."

"I have a name already," I say quietly. It's silvery, quick and shining, delicate and perfect, a name to conjure wading pools, rivers, and smooth stones. But I don't say all that. "I'm going to call her Minnow."

"Minnow?" Dr. Nancy repeats. Her expression says she thinks she's heard me wrong.

"Yes." I look down at my sneakers, feeling like your name is a secret I've told and want to take back.

After I leave Dr. Nancy's office, I look for some place cool to grab a bite, but there aren't any restaurants or cafés in the neighborhood. Years later, the Flatiron District becomes super commercial, full of restaurants, a farmers' market, and every retail store you can think of, but at the time it's industrial, desolate, and kind of dirty. A lot of photographers have their studios here in the soot-covered loft buildings. Garbage blows through the streets as it does in much of New York City in the eighties. I look down Sixth Avenue to the bottom of Manhattan and see the twin towers of the World Trade Center.

By the time I reach Ray's Original Pizza, on the corner of Eleventh Street, I'm dripping in sweat. I order a Coke and a slice and snag one of the few tables. The air conditioner is blasting, but every time someone comes through the door, they bring a gust of hot air in with them.

I take your Polaroid from my bag and place it beside me on

the table. I want to show it to someone, even to the strangers at Ray's. I wish Gabriel were with me. I think of the friends I've lost touch with since I've been with him, and identify the ache I feel as loneliness. When an incoming gust sends your picture flying, I make a grab for it, and put you away safely in my pocket.

Outside, the sky grows dark through the plate glass. A skinny weed-tree blows back and forth. By the time I've finished my pizza, it's pouring out, the kind of teeming rain that only happens in the extreme heat of summer. I pull up my collar and make a run for the subway.

Once, when I was about fourteen, after a fight with my mother, I ran out of the house into a summer storm like this one. It was just getting dark outside. I don't recall the argument itself, or my mother's shrieking voice, which surely would have demanded I return at once. What I remember is running barefoot, as fast as I could, rain pouring down, the sound of my rapid breath, the slap of my feet on the black tar street. At the end of a dead-end road, there was a high Cyclone fence that overlooked the expressway, and I started to climb it. Cars were rushing by. I was crying so hard, I couldn't tell the rain from my tears.

All of a sudden it occurred to me that the hurtful things my parents said didn't matter. I hung there listening to the sound of the rain in the trees, watching the red taillights speed away, and thought about how it was powerful, natural forces that ruled the world, not my parents, and that one day I was going to be free of them and everything would be different.

Now I bound down the subway stairs dripping wet. On the train, I find your picture in my pocket and dry it off with my inside sleeve.

There you are, Minnow. Proof.

Fourteen

The new apartment is in the back of a town house on West Seventy-first Street, between Broadway and West End Avenue. It has a nice kitchen, with a small butcher-block island, that takes up a whole wall of the main room. Through a Dutch door in back there's a garden that's not a garden, exactly, but a yard full of broken concrete and rocks. The narrow bedroom has a window with a view of a scraggly sapling, the only tree in the yard. The whole apartment is probably no more than five hundred square feet in all. Still, it's twice the size of the Seventy-eighth Street studio. It feels like a real home to me.

I move in August, with no furniture except for the crib, changing table, and other baby things. I set up the bedroom for you as a nursery, make curtains for the window, paint a mural of the solar system on one wall and a girl flying a kite on another. Maybe you'll dream of flying, as I did when I was a girl. It's been a long time since I could fly in my dreams, but I can clearly recall the way it felt to lift off, and up, to glide over the rooftops of my neighborhood. Imagine what it would be like to fly over New York City? What views! The Metropolitan Museum of Art glowing next to the dark trees of Central Park, sailboats on the East River, the bright lights and billboards of Times Square. I'd like to fly over it with you.

Here on earth, I paint and clean and fix things—doing it now because soon I'll be too pregnant, and it will be impossible. I'm right on schedule. *Your Baby* says now is the time for making the nest.

I pick up the rest of the furnishings at the flea market on Twenty-sixth Street and Sixth Avenue. I find an old wicker daybed, a walnut dresser, a long table with three pine boards,

and a red rocking chair. I face the rocker toward the window
and place a soft blanket on its back, imagining it wrapped
around us in the middle of the night.

I buy plants for the garden, too, but the job of cleaning it
out is too much for me. I don't even consider asking Gabriel for
help. Even before he began to avoid me, he would have found a
way to avoid yard work. I call my friends Jules and Alan, and
they agree to come over and give me a hand.

Jules and Alan have been my closest friends for almost
as long as I've been in New York City. They are the family
I made when I left home, the ones who will sing to you and
bring you presents, make you laugh and watch you grow up.
The two share the same birthday, a year apart, and although
they only know one another through me, the coincidence
makes them feel related. I haven't seen much of either one
since I've been with Gabriel, but they understand that, or
say they do.

Alan is a guitar player. I met him in school. We used to cut
class together and walk around the city talking about music.
He's very opinionated and cool, but if he's your friend, it's for
life. He's funny, too. Once, I was drinking milk and he made
me laugh so hard it came out of my nose.

Jules also has a good sense of humor, although there's something almost regal about her. Maybe it's the high forehead or
her clear gray eyes. She's even smarter than she is beautiful,
always hungry to learn more about philosophy, mythology, or
art history. She's a little full of herself, but so would you be, if
you were a brilliant actress on the cusp of becoming a movie
star. One time, before we really knew one another, we discovered we were dating the same man. We compared notes,
ditched him, and became best friends.

The three of us begin cleaning out the garden around noon,

and hardly take a break all day. It's grueling work to rake out all those rocks. We fill garbage bags to bursting with debris and drag them out to the curb. The cats follow us out back. They stretch their long bodies in the sun and scratch on the old fencing. It's a hot summer day and the sweat pours off us, but we have fun, too. We catch up, talk about our latest adventures and mishaps.

By five o'clock, we're so giddy with fatigue and hunger that everything strikes us funny. We laugh so hard, we have to stop to hold our stomachs and wipe our eyes.

"I'm starving," says Jules.

"Me, too," I say.

Alan takes a look at the contents of my fridge and decides he can make spaghetti Bolognese. He loves to cook. We think if he wanted to, he could be a chef. Jules and I watch him chop the pathetic onion and lone garlic clove he finds in the crisper. He combines a couple of hamburger patties and simmers it all together. The smell makes our mouths water.

We put whatever money we've got together, a few crumpled dollar bills and some change, and I make a run to get wine. Alan and Jules drag the table outside to the newly cleared yard, and we set it with candles and my mother's cloth napkins. It's a warm August evening. I tell myself it's a night I will never forget, and maybe that's what makes it so.

"To the little rock star," Alan says, and we lift our glasses to you. I barely let the wine touch my lips.

Then we make a toast to Jules, to wish her luck. She's up for a big movie, and is anxiously awaiting a call from her agent. Last summer she was cast in an independent horror film about monsters in the subway tunnels. But this one would be huge. It has a big budget and a famous director. She tells us it's shooting in London in the fall.

I'm jealous. I'd like to have exciting career things happen to me, too. Alan and I talk about starting a band, but it's hard to imagine what life will be like once you're born. Will there be time to do anything else?

After dinner, Alan takes my Martin from its stand and plays us an instrumental he's working on. I sing along, making up words as I go. Jules attempts to join in with a harmony, although she's not really a singer. The song gets sillier and sillier until we're just laughing. Alan is yipping and barking like a dog.

"We should record that!" he says.

Fifteen

In the original 1982, my songs start to fill me with ambition. I want to hear them on the radio. I want to sing them with a band behind me. Drums and bass, piano, cello, accordion, trumpet. Alan and I get together all the time and practice. I'm less than confident about my guitar playing, so I teach him my songs, and he transforms them from folk songs into R&B ballads, rock songs, and bossa novas.

There's a big songwriter scene at the time on Bleecker Street. We go down there one Monday night and sign up for the open mic at Folk City. After we play our two songs, Stevie, the owner of the club, approaches us. "That was really good, you guys," he says. "You want to play a night here? I've got a Sunday open middle of the month."

Yeah, we do. We talk about what we should wear for days.

We assemble the rest of a band and book a rehearsal space to practice. I make flyers to leave all over town and mail to everyone I know.

I have photographs from that first gig. I'm wearing a headband like Madonna circa 1981. Alan looks handsome, his long hair is falling over one eye. Fish is playing keyboards. He played with a lot of up-and-coming singer-songwriters at the time. That's Mildred, from Gabriel's band, on backing vocals. Look how young she was. Her round, brown eyes are on me as she matches my phrasing, word for word.

We begin to play pretty regularly at Folk City and the other small clubs on or around Bleecker Street. I have terrible stage fright. Sometimes I shake so hard, I can barely hold my fingers on the strings. Alan covers for me and usually by the third song in I'm okay. We add a drummer and bass player, once in a while a guy on sax.

Gabriel comes down to the club and sits at the bar. It feels good to have my own thing, to have him come to hear *me* play for a change, although when I look over at him from the stage, he's usually talking to some stranger and doesn't seem to be paying attention. Still, he gives me notes about one thing or another. He thinks my songs are too slow, and I should add some up-tempo material to the set. He thinks I should cover Michael Jackson, maybe, or the Police. But I only play my own songs. Every one is about him. One is called "Part of the World." It's about the fact that Gabriel's concerns are worldwide, while mine are only for the world we make between us. The refrain goes like this:

> *I, too, want to save the world*
> *The part that's yours and mine*

Thankfully, it's been lost to posterity.

I didn't really become a good songwriter until many years later. It takes a long time and a lot of practice to do something well.

But enough of the old stories, Little Fish.

Sixteen

You kick him so hard, it knocks his hand right off my belly. Gabriel looks truly shocked, eyes wide, mouth agape. *"¡Coño!"* he says, laughing. "She's gonna be a boxer. Is that normal?"

I laugh, too. I'm so happy to have him share in the amazement. "She's pretty energetic," I say. "I think she's swimming laps in there."

"You're gonna have to name her after Manny," he says. Manuel "Manny" Luís is a famous fighter from Gabriel's country. "Easy there, champ," he says to you as you give him another little kick.

After that, it's what he calls you. "How's the Champ?" he asks when he calls or stops by on his way downtown. His accent makes the *ch* sound sort of like a *sh*.

He makes my apartment feel small when he's there, makes me feel messy and a little ashamed. Within five minutes of his arrival my clothes are off and we're on the wicker daybed, his pants dropped around his ankles.

Afterward, he's ready to go. "I can't stay long," he always says. "The guys are waiting for me. You okay? Need anything? Need some money?"

I pull my pants back on and button my shirt. I fear I'm no longer pretty enough to hold his attention.

He takes a roll of bills from his pocket, peels off a twenty, and places it on the table. "Gotta go, kid," he says. "Let me know if you need anything. Maybe a movie this week?"

Your father is a tornado of energy. He's got a million projects in the works. He's always on his way somewhere to promote himself, or meet with somebody to talk about a new opportunity. He flies to L.A. to take some meetings. A guy from Warner Bros. wants him to make a record in English. There's talk about a movie. He does an interview and a photo shoot for *Rolling Stone*.

Does he think of you as a ticking time bomb, an expiration date on his freedom? Does he think of you at all? Does he imagine he'll escape us, somehow, find a way to outsmart us, trick us into never needing him?

Seventeen

In late September we rent folding chairs and set them up outside. The forecast has called for rain, but so far there's no sign of it. In the garden, a weeping cherry tree sits in the center of the small lawn I've planted. Flower beds along the fence are full of goldenrod and mums. There's a delicate rose or two in final bloom.

Alan has come early to help me set up for the baby shower. He's brought a dozen frosted cupcakes, and we've already eaten half. Miki, a waitress friend who's started her own catering company, drops by with tea sandwiches of cucumber, cream cheese, and dark bread. We set out a colorful bowl of fruit on the butcher-block counter.

My mother arrives with my sister, Lynn, up from Miami for the weekend. Her dark hair is curling in the New York humidity. She's a dead ringer for my dad, who's dropped them off and gone home. They've brought more food and a shopping bag full of decorations. My sister tells me what she's been up to as we go through the contents. She's working for a travel magazine now. She gets to go to honeymoon destinations and stay in beautiful hotels. The only weird thing about it, she says, is having her dinner alone in a dining room full of newlyweds.

Alan follows me out to the garden with a roll of streamers. We wrap the fence in pink and yellow. The cats sit in the grass and watch, waiting to make the colorful strips of paper their toy.

I think of Jules, far away. She won't be coming to the shower. She's gotten the lead in the big movie and is already shooting in London. She's called to say she's homesick. She misses her dog and her bed. They've cut her hair off, short as a boy's, and she hates it. "You can't imagine the drama." She laughs. She does that, laughs after describing things that upset her, as if to emphasize the absurdity.

"I'm sure it will get better."

"I don't know. It's very political and everyone knows everyone. I'm the only outsider."

Still, I'm jealous.

My mother's sister, Aunt Lou, arrives, carrying a big box wrapped in a pink bow. My cousin Rachel is right behind her; she's a year older than my sister and looks more like my mother than we do. Sofia and Nina from work follow, wearing flowery summer dresses. Other friends arrive.

"What an adorable apartment," they say. "Look at you! How are you feeling?"

"I can no longer see my feet," I tell them happily.

Everyone smiles and holds their open hands against my high round belly, to feel you roll and kick. They ask about your name and stand in the nursery, admiring the murals. We envision your tiny person in the crib against the far wall. I'm already proud to be your mother.

They ask about Gabriel, too. He's been in the paper recently, the *New York Times* Arts & Leisure section. The headline read CROSSOVER KING. He's promised to make an appearance at some point today, as much as he hates these things.

I put off opening gifts for as long as possible, but when he hasn't come by three, we start without him. We gather on the lawn, everyone seated around me. My sister places each wrapped gift in my hands, and I open it, trying not to tear the pretty paper. We ooh and aah over every miniature article of clothing and pass it along to be inspected by everyone in the circle. It's a well-practiced ritual, exact in its specificity. At the end, every item is returned to its box, accompanied by a card, to remind me of whom to thank for what.

When it starts to rain, it's getting late by then anyway. We quickly gather all the presents and wrapping and move inside. I call the cats in, and they come running back, from over the fence where they go.

After most everyone has gone, and only my mother, sister, and Alan remain, Gabriel shows up.

"Hi," he says. "Sorry I'm late. Did I miss the whole party?"

"What a shame you couldn't be here," my mother says. "Such a wonderful day." She's mad at him, though it's hard to tell through her characteristic cheerfulness. I'm almost seven months pregnant and there's been no offer to put a ring on my finger.

Gabriel is oblivious to her message. "I know. I tried to get here sooner. These guys can talk your head off."

I have to smile because although I don't know where he's been, I know he was the one doing the talking. He sits beside me and puts his arm around me.

"Sorry I'm late, baby." He kisses my cheek.

My mother is picking up discarded plates and napkins, bits of tape, ribbon, and wrapping paper. Gabriel jumps up to take the garbage bag from her hands. "Let me do that, Mrs. Nelson."

She warms to him then, just a little. Maybe she thinks it means a proposal is near. He picks up a napkin, a cup, and sets the bag down.

"Hey, nice article in the paper, man," Alan says.

"Oh, you saw that? Thanks, man!" Gabriel is in good spirits. I'm feeling pretty good, too. I'm thinking about leftovers, planning what I'll eat first after everyone has gone home. All I want to do is eat and sleep, but I'm glad Gabriel is there. I feel a hopefulness about us. Maybe it will all work out somehow. When he smiles at me, I beam my love at him full blast, and it makes him laugh.

"Pajarito," he says tenderly.

Eighteen

When I first hear the rumor, I dismiss it instantly. I know it can't be true. It hurts to hear the vile lie, makes me a little nauseous, but he would never, ever, do that to me. I know he wouldn't.

Gabriel's been spending more and more time in L.A. He says that's where the opportunity is. He calls me every night, though. He tells me how much he misses me. We make plans for when he's back in town. He seems happy again, in fact, accepting of impending fatherhood. He brings me little presents. He's always full of stories. So, it's not possible that what I hear is true. No way.

Janelle is such a gossip, I think. Why doesn't she worry about her own life for a change? Why does she always have her nose in everyone else's business?

"I heard it from a very reliable source," she says gently. We're all sitting around the table in the back of the restaurant where we eat before out shift. She's speaking to me like I'm a mental patient, like I might totally flip out.

I want to slap her face, wipe the sympathy right off it. What does she know about the love we share? She doesn't even know us. Look at her. She's never been less attractive. She's getting old; she must be nearly thirty.

"You don't know what you're talking about," I say. Then I stand up, throw my apron off, and storm out of the restaurant.

My heart is beating in my ears. I'm walking so fast, the people I pass are a blur. I go straight to his building. I walk past the doorman and get in the elevator, push three. I still have my key. If it were true, wouldn't he have taken back the key? Gabriel, no, I'm thinking. Please, no. Don't let it be true.

Though he's in town, he isn't home. I let myself in.

I stand in the kitchen and look around the place. I notice one strange thing right off the bat. The couch has been turned to face the fireplace. That's when I know that what Janelle said might be true. The couch facing the fireplace fills me with dread. I go over to it and sit down. It looks east now. Through the window, I can see Central Park. The trees are beginning to turn yellow.

I get up and go into his office. You have to climb two steps and pass through French doors. I sit at his desk and open one drawer, and then the next. I'm not surprised to find evidence of all the others, photographs, postcards, and little notes he's saved. What do I expect to find that will confirm it? I open a notebook in the second drawer. It's filled with lyrics written in English. He's been writing songs for the English album. I look for clues in the words he's chosen. Some are love songs, but what does that prove?

In the bedroom closet, I go through the pockets of his jackets. He has a lot of them. Baseball jackets, blazers, cashmere and leather coats. I look at the names of restaurants on matchbooks. I check the addresses on crumpled receipts.

The phone rings, and I jump. I let it ring again before answering it.

"Hello?" I say tentatively.

"Hi," Gabriel says. He's startled to hear my voice. "I was just calling for my messages."

"Gabriel," I say.

"What's wrong, baby?" He sounds worried. He loves me. I know he does.

"I heard something really bad."

"What did you hear?"

"I can't even say it, it's so terrible."

"Is everything okay with the baby? Is your family all right?"

"Everyone's fine," I say. "It isn't that."

"What is it, then?" he asks carefully.

"It's about you," I say.

He's quiet then.

"Just stay there," he says. "I'll be home in an hour. Okay? I'll be there as soon as I can."

I hang up the phone and sit on the bed. This room is the world I would live in if I could. I wouldn't care if everything else evaporated, if I could only stay here with him.

But it's slipping away from me.

I place my hands over my belly and lie back on the bed. I look up at the white ceiling.

Little Fish, I told you he breaks my heart.

When I was a little girl, I used to talk to God this way, lying on my back in bed. I would look right up through the ceiling, as if God were a kind man just on the other side of it, as if His ear rested on the roof and His eyes could look through it to see me. I wasn't raised with any religion, so I'm not sure where this idea came from, but it was a great comfort to me as a child, to feel His presence there. As I talked to him, the tears would fall sideways from my eyes onto my pillow, even if what I had to tell him wasn't especially sad. It was being listened to that made me cry.

Gabriel gets home soon after. I hear his key in the lock; he says my name, finds me lying on the bed. He climbs onto it beside me, and we hold each other, not saying anything.

"What did you hear?" he asks finally.

"I heard you got married in California," I say quietly.

"Who told you that?" He wants to know so he can seek revenge. He'd like to kill whoever told me.

"Is it true?" I ask.

"I was going to tell you," he says. "It's not what it sounds like. There's a good explanation."

I wait for it, the big lie sure to follow. Does he even know how to tell the truth? But perhaps this is too big even for a champion liar like him.

"It has nothing to do with how much I love you, Pajarito," he says. "It just happened. I met someone. It just happened."

"But you said you didn't want to get married," I say to him. "How could you marry her instead of me? How could you just meet someone and marry her, just like that?"

He covers his face with his hands. He's actually crying.

"I'm so sorry," he says. "I didn't want to hurt you. I feel terrible. You know I'll always love you."

"But you're someone else's husband now," I say.

That's when I should get up and walk out the door, but that's not what happens. Instead, we undress one another and make love for the rest of the afternoon. The whole time, we cry and cry.

Later that week, he packs his overnight bag and leaves for L.A.

I see the announcement in the *New York Times*. His wife is a leggy beauty, a former model. In one more blow, the paper refers to her as his longtime love. She has a name similar to my own and they mistake us for the same person. Reading it, I feel as if he's taken everything that matters away from me, even the history we share.

Nineteen

Little Fish, when you lose someone you love, the color drains out of the world. Sounds seem muffled and far away. Your reaction to things happens in slow motion.

I feel Gabriel's eyes on me the way some feel watched by God. I hear his opinions about every thought in my head.

There are constant reminders: favorite songs and restaurants, baseball games, boxing matches, parking garages, lottery tickets, the scent of frying onions. His new record is being promoted, too, so there are pictures of him in magazines and an advertisement at the bus stop. He's on TV being interviewed by Geraldo Rivera. It feels like the whole world has taken his side and left me behind to fill an unfillable emptiness.

At first, he still calls at odd hours. He promises he's coming back to see me. When finally he does, we meet at his apartment. Before the door is even completely closed, he's pushing my head down trying to get me to give him a blow job, and I know it's his way of being loyal to his wife. She's the one who hears now, "This is only for you, Mami."

I refuse to do it and he gets mad.

I try not to obsess about his wife. I've seen pictures of her. She's a sultry blonde with wide-set eyes and long muscular legs. I keep seeing some part of her when I look at him, her long leg wrapped around his waist, her downturned mouth against his throat. I see her influence in the way he dresses. New words and expressions fall out of his mouth. As I listen to him talk, all I can hear is how I've lost him.

It's almost a relief when I leave Gabriel's apartment and return to mine.

After that, he stops calling.

The nights are the hardest. I can't sleep or I have bad dreams. In one, I beat his chest in a rage, but he can't even feel me. I cry my eyes raw. I wake up at three or four, and remember all over again. I lie awake, waiting for the sky to get light.

I'm afraid my misery will bleed into you, and I don't want that to happen. I hope you'll be stronger than I am, capable and brave, that you'll feel a bit of the entitlement your father sees as his birthright. It's an easier life for him.

Twenty

Weeks later I'm under the covers at three in the afternoon when someone rings the bell. My heart starts to pound; I'm not expecting anyone. I pull the pillow over my head and try to ignore it, but it sounds again. So reluctantly I get out of bed and say into the intercom, "Who is it?" My voice comes out whispery and ragged.

"You sleeping?" Alan asks.

I pull on my sweats and buzz him in.

He laughs when he sees me. Not in a mean way. I do look a sight. My hair is standing straight up and I haven't bathed or brushed my teeth in days. I'm huge, too. It's unbelievable that I've still got a month to go, because I look ready to pop at any moment.

Alan seems happy to see me, which makes me feel a little bit better. He launches into a story about a girl on the subway who smiled at him from Grand Central all the way to Seventy-second Street, but turned out to be smiling at someone else. The other guy, muscle-bound and from Jersey, asked Alan if he'd like a punch in the mouth.

"No way," I say. "Did that really happen?"

"Oh, yes," Alan says. "It happened all right."

"What did you do?"

"I said, no thank you, and got the hell off the train," he says, and we laugh. It feels really good to laugh. I realize I've gone five minutes without thinking about Gabriel.

"Anyhow," Alan says, the story trailing off. "So, you all right?"

I look around the room. It's a total mess. "Do you think you could hang out while I clean up a little?" I ask.

"Sure," he says easily. He moves across the room toward my guitar.

I take a quick shower and start to put the place in order. It doesn't take very long. Alan follows me to the kitchen looking for something to eat, but the cupboard is bare. The cats are on his heels, hoping he'll fill up their bowl. "I have to eat," he says. "Do you want to get something at the corner, or should we buy stuff and cook?"

We decide to cook, and do a quick shop at the Korean deli on Broadway. I feed the cats, and he makes us a couple of omelets with goat cheese and spinach. We toast a loaf of French bread in the broiler and break off big buttery hunks of it to stuff in our mouths. We drink fresh-squeezed orange juice and cut up a melon into large wedges. It's the first real meal I've had in weeks and I'm stuffed.

"If Minnow's not like fifteen pounds, I'm in trouble," I say, leaning back in my chair.

"You're not so fat," Alan says.

"What's happening with music?" I ask him, changing the subject.

He says there may be some session work coming up. Ideally, he'd like to find a tour. Paul Simon is reuniting with Art Garfunkel, but another guitar player we know seems to have that locked up. Chaka Khan might be looking for somebody. Alan knows her musical director. He grabs the guitar to play some funky licks. I think he'd be perfect for her band.

"Have you been writing at all?" he asks me.

"Not really," I say.

But after he leaves I pick up the guitar. It's comforting to slip into my own world, safe and dark and full of caves to explore. I don't need Gabriel, I tell myself. My talent will be discovered and I'll be rewarded with recognition, love, and approval. It might happen anywhere, at any time. The thought consoles me. I don't have the slightest clue that it's a childish dream.

Twenty-one

On Halloween the streets are filled with children dressed as little ghouls and princesses. I smile and wave to them as they go by the restaurant. One little girl rides on her father's shoulders, her black curls bouncing, her crown askew. She laughs and her black-fringed eyes sparkle. Minnow, will you burst with happiness like that girl? I see you in every beautiful child's face.

All the waitresses at the Café Miriam are in costume, too. I'm wearing cat ears. I've painted whiskers on my face and a black nose. I've got on a black body stocking and a tail. My pregnant belly seems part of my costume. I'm a mother cat about to birth a dozen kittens.

My fellow waitresses are sexy gypsies and nurses. Only Will, the bartender, conceals his identity. He is the Tin Man from *The Wizard of Oz*. He'd make a better lion, I think, with his barrel chest. He's mixing drinks with his arms encased in silver cardboard. It doesn't look easy.

Toward the middle of the afternoon, there's a lull, and we're all standing around the bar talking and teasing him.

Sofia says, "Uh-oh."

And I look around.

Gabriel is coming through the door. Did I mention he liked

to wear hats? Before he got married and moved to L.A., it was baseball caps. Now it's a black fedora, tilted sideways on his head. I can tell he thinks it makes him look cool. Plus it hides his bald spot.

I meet his eyes and his gaze travels down to my belly. In my catsuit, there is nothing left to the imagination. He looks surprised, maybe a little nervous. I'm as big as a house now.

"He's got a lot of nerve coming in here," Janelle says under her breath.

But she's the only one who says anything. We're all waiting to see what he's going to do. Nobody even asks him if he wants a table. He looks at us, staring back at him. We must look pretty silly, all in costume. For a second he's got the beginnings of a smile on his face, but then it falls, and he turns around and walks back out.

Part of me wants to follow him down the street, but I stay where I am. I get a big lump in my throat that dissolves into tears. Sofia dabs at my face with a cocktail napkin. "Don't cry," she says. "He's not worth it, and you're going to mess up your whiskers."

I smile when she says that, but for the rest of the day he's the only thought in my head. I wonder if he's at the apartment. I wonder how long he'll be in town. I wonder if he misses me. Still, I don't go to his place and I don't call him. This may be the hardest thing I've ever done. I feel like an addict craving the drug. But I've started to realize that the longer I stay away from him, the easier it gets.

In the original 1982, I lose my mind. I drink myself into oblivion. I call him repeatedly and wait outside his door. I beg him to tell me why.

He grows bored with my drunken pain.

"I've told you why," he says.

"But I don't remember," I say, sobbing.

"Well, maybe you should write it down."

But there's no way it's going to happen like that this time. I'm pregnant. I don't drink. I don't call. I don't wait outside his door.

I leave the restaurant in the late afternoon. There's a light rain falling. I hold my face up to it and close my eyes. It seems to always rain on Halloween.

I get home in time for all the little trick-or-treaters in the neighborhood. I'm ready for them. I pretend to be afraid. I tell them they look scary or beautiful or funny.

They hold bags open, already full of candy, and say, "Trick or treat!"

I drop Hershey's Kisses and miniature Milky Way bars into the bags of ghosts and mermaids, superheroes, and clowns. Their parents stand a few steps behind, under half-open umbrellas. The mothers ask me when I'm due. Their smiles are welcoming.

Twenty-two

Alan comes with me to prenatal class. We make fun of everything. I don't think any of the other women look as pregnant as I do. They're mostly in their thirties. One is even in her forties. They seem superior and smug to me in their expensive spandex outfits, their well-groomed husbands in tow.

The woman who leads the class, Nicole, reminds me of an elegant racehorse. She says our babies will grow a lot in the last month and Alan and I look at each other with raised eyebrows and laugh. How is that possible? Already, I'm waddling like a beast. I've outgrown my maternity clothes. I can't find a comfortable position in which to sleep.

One woman says she sleeps with eight pillows. Another says yoga has saved her life. I listen to everyone but feel I have nothing in common with these people.

Thank God Alan is with me. When we're shown a video of a birth, he covers his eyes with his hands. I do, too, but peek through my fingers. I know somehow you've got to come out, but I can't believe this is the way it still happens. You'd think with all the advances in technology and science, they'd have come up with something less barbaric by now.

Nicole talks about preparing for the hospital, what to pack in our bags, and when to know it's time. She describes the pain management options and has us practice breathing. I fear I'm too distracted to remember half of what she says; I'm going to miss something important. But a woman who is having her second baby says no matter what you learn beforehand, once the baby starts coming, you don't remember a thing anyway.

"That's why we have our wonderful husbands with us today," Nicole says.

I look at Alan and he smiles at me like a goofball. People in the class assume he's my husband. Someone calls us a cute couple. He reaches out to pat me on the head, and I smack his hand away. I don't know why I don't love him like that. He's the best friend I have and I count on him for so much.

The light is long and yellow as we walk back to my place. It's a late November afternoon. Alan wants to stop for ice cream cones, so we do. We get brown bonnets. The chocolate shell cracks and falls apart faster than I can keep up. Soon I've got ice cream running down my arm.

At the apartment, I take my guitar out of Alan's hands.

"I've got a new one," I tell him, holding the guitar awkwardly. My belly prevents my cradling it normally. The song is called "Still True."

> *Baby, all I've ever looked for is a safe place,*
> *All I've ever longed for is your warm embrace,*
> *All I've ever wanted is you.*
> *Take a good look and you'll know*
> *It's still true*

"Damn. That's a nice one." The cats are at Alan's feet. He reaches up from scratching their heads to take the guitar from my hands.

"You could play it this way." He starts to strum it.

"Oh, I love that." I sing the melody over the song's new feel. It's got that eighth note in the bass thing now, like a lot of songs in the years after "Every Breath You Take." We play it a few times through.

"I definitely hear cello on it," I say.

This is before we knew Marianne Mercurio, the cellist who one day plays on "Still True" and many of my other songs. In the original 1982, I go to CBGB's to see Shelly Lee Rowan play and Marianne is with her. She's sitting on the right side of the stage, cello between her legs, wearing a black leather cap. Her long straight hair swings back and forth with every frenetic push and pull of her bow. I think she's the coolest girl I've ever seen. Years later, when we're making the first record, my producer tracks her down. This is back in the day of big-budget records, before the majors ran out of money.

Marianne becomes the third member of our band.

"Yeah, cello would be extremely cool," Alan says now.

Twenty-three

My parents come into town and take me to lunch at the coffee shop on Broadway. They love diners and coffee shops because there's a lot to choose from and the food is predictable and inexpensive. BLTs and spinach pie, meatloaf sandwiches, and tuna melts.

As a young family, we sometimes attempted to go to other restaurants. My father would tell us that we shouldn't drink the water or eat the bread before he'd looked at the menu, because if the prices were too high, we were going to leave. It had actually happened more than once, and we'd walked out, trailing behind him feeling mildly humiliated. When my sister got to be a teenager, she got him back by always ordering a lobster or a sirloin steak.

My father reads his menu now and doesn't say much. In fact, he says nothing at all about the enormous elephant in the room, his soon-to-be-born granddaughter. I can barely fit behind the table in the booth, but it's as if he doesn't notice. At first, my mother fills the space with small talk about distant relatives I barely know or remember. When my father interrupts her, she stops midsentence.

"Lise," he says, "what's your plan?"

"What do you mean, Dad?" I ask.

"Obviously, you're not going to be able to keep doing what you've been doing once the baby is born," he says.

"Why not?" I ask, dreading the answer.

But he ignores my question. "Your mother and I think you should move back home. It's time to get serious about your life. We've let this go on too long already."

"Dad, I'm twenty-four years old," I say. Though instantly I feel sixteen, defiant and doubting myself.

The waiter interrupts to ask for our order. My voice shakes with emotion as I give him mine.

But I have a job. I have a place to live. I have money in the bank. I know it won't be easy to take care of a baby on my own, but other single women have managed it and so will I.

After the waiter walks away, I tell him that.

"Dad, it's going to be fine. I've thought it all out. I can do this."

He doesn't believe me. Of course he doesn't. I understand the deal I'm making. He looks at me as if from a long distance. If this is what I choose, then there's nothing he can do. The consequences will be mine, and they won't be pretty. It's a hard life I'm making for myself. All of this is in his eyes.

"Look, here's our food," my mother says. "Doesn't everything look good?"

I'm too upset to eat and stare out the window. My mother resumes chatting, as if nothing has been said. I feel bad and then worse.

The waiter comes by and asks if anyone needs more coffee.

"No, thank you," my mother answers for us.

"I have to go," I say. "I have to be at work by four."

"How can you be on your feet in your condition?" she asks.

"I'm hostessing. It's not so bad."

I waddle around to their side of the table to kiss them good-bye.

"We can drop you off," my mother says. "Let Dad get the car. It won't take a minute."

"I feel like walking." I kiss my mother's cheek and pull

away before she can kiss mine. I head out the door into the cold afternoon.

With every block I put between them and myself, I feel better.

Twenty-four

Later, at the Café Miriam, I've got the big reservation book open in front of me. I'm greeting customers and seating a few people. It's a pretty slow night, so mostly I'm just watching them walk by the restaurant.

Hostessing is a breeze compared to waiting tables, though the money isn't as good. Most people don't think to tip me as I seat them. The ones who do are older women who take pity on me because I'm pregnant, but never give more than a dollar. If I weren't pregnant, it would be married men doing the tipping, slipping a five into my palm, as if I were a stripper and my hand a G-string. They think it's a subtle way to get your attention, and that their wives don't notice. News flash, guys? Not very subtle, and your wives don't miss a thing.

In my current state, the married men hardly look at me. Not only because I'm pregnant. I've also lost the sheen of love, that happiness you radiate when you love someone and he loves you back. The wives still look me up and down to assess the wardrobe (man's button-down shirt over a pair of black maternity stretch pants). I see them glance at my left hand to check for a ring.

I'm still feeling disoriented after the lunch with my parents. Or maybe it's you, Minnow. I'm a little dizzy, a bit sick to my stomach. But I get through the shift. At least I don't have to wait around until the money's figured out and everything's cleaned up, as I would if I were waitressing. After the last customer is seated, I hang out at the bar for a few minutes, have a Coke with Will, and say good night to the girls. By ten-fifteen, I'm on my way home.

The perspiration at my hairline cools in the chilly night. Being pregnant is like having a heater in my belly; I'm always too warm. My bones ache and I'm tired, but I walk briskly. Columbus Avenue is alive with people spilling out of all the bars and restaurants. They laugh and push one another, drunkenly. I cut over to Amsterdam.

West Seventy-first Street is desolate as I approach my building just before West End Avenue. I can hear my own breathing and footsteps in the quiet. I dig through my bag for my front door key and go to turn it in the lock. I'm just about to get inside when someone grabs my arm and spins me around.

The guy facing me looks deranged. He's a street person, definitely a drug addict. I don't understand how he's managed to sneak up on me.

I don't fight him as he roughly pulls my bag off my shoulder. He pushes me hard, and I fall back and down, against the front door. He takes my wallet out of the bag and throws the rest onto the sidewalk.

"Do you have any jewelry?" he asks.

"No," I say, but no sound comes out.

"Bitch," he says. His eyes are popping out of his head. I try to keep my own head down. "That's right. Don't look at me. And don't get up. Sit there and count to a hundred before you go inside or I'll come back and cut you." His saliva strikes my arm. I think of the phrase *spitting mad.* I don't look at him.

"Say 'okay'!" He commands.

"Okay." My voice is barely audible. My head is down. He walks off and I start counting. I get to seventy before I look up. He's gone but I finish counting. I get up slowly, gather my things from the sidewalk, and go inside. That's when I notice my pants are soaking wet. At first I think I've peed myself, but then I realize that my water has broken. I think about whether I should call the police to report the mugging or an ambulance to take me to the hospital. I remember my insurance card is in the wallet.

I'll go to the hospital. I'm shaking as I dial 911. "I need an ambulance, please." I give the operator my address.

I call Dr. Nancy and tell her answering service that I'm on my way.

I call Alan and tell him, too.

I try to reach my parents, but their phone rings and rings.

I pour out a couple of bowls of food for the cats and refill their water.

The buzzer sounds. The ambulance has arrived. I don't have a bag packed. I have no wallet, and I've just been mugged. Still, all I can think about is that soon I am going to meet you, Minnow.

I lock up the apartment and go out to the ambulance. They have me lie down on a stretcher. Take my blood pressure and my temperature. They close the doors.

"Are you going to turn on the siren?" I ask the driver.

"Sure," he says. He's kind of cute.

The siren begins to wail as we take off. Speeding across town, to get you born.

Part 2

Minnow

Twenty-five

On a late November morning, in a chilly delivery room lit by overhead fluorescents, at an East Side hospital, after eight and a half hours of labor, the older nurse, the one with the Polish accent, says: "One, two . . . Push, Lisa, now *push*."

I push through the count of ten, and rest.

"Good," she says.

Then we do it again, and again.

I cry for my mother. I hold on to the nurse so tightly her fingers turn white. I keep waking from a dream and falling back into it. I can't tell the difference between dreaming and being awake. The contractions come closer and faster. The hands on the wall clock don't seem to move. I'm aware of Dr. Diamond's voice, the green and blue scrubs, the circular overhead light. Later, it will be hard to remember any of it.

I'm given an epidural for the pain, but by then, I'm so tired.

"I can't," I say weakly.

But they say I can.

"Keep breathing. Keep pushing. Good. Good."

"One more time. That's right. Now push!"

Finally, the doctor says, "Here we go."

The first thing I see is your tiny hand like a star. You come out, arms waving, and let out a cry.

Dr. Diamond cuts the thick blue cord with a pair of scissors, and smiles down at me. He looks tired. "You did good, kid," he says.

"You, too, Doctor," I say, and they laugh. I can't believe they do this every day.

I feel the awe of it, nature, or God, or whatever it is we're all a part of.

The other nurse, the young one, cleans you of the afterbirth and puts you on a scale. "Six pounds three ounces," she tells me.

"How is she?" I ask, reaching for you.

"She's perfect," the young nurse says. I'm filled with love for her round, angelic face as she places you across my chest.

"She looks like a plum," I say, exhausted, delirious. I don't want to ever let you go, but then the older nurse, the one with the Polish accent, is taking you from me, and I can't remember what happens next. I guess I fall asleep.

Twenty-six

Late that afternoon (how can it still be the same day?) my parents and Alan crowd the hospital bed. My sister has already come and gone. She's on her way back to Miami, where she has to work in the morning. My father seems happy. I think I see a tear in his eye.

We marvel at the miracle of you. Your eyelashes. Your toes. The perfect shape of your head. I see Gabriel in the line of your brow and your Cupid's-bow lips. I close my eyes and send him a telepathic message: *She's born.* I have no doubt that one day he will meet you and be amazed.

Late at night, after everyone has gone, another nurse brings you to me and leaves you in my arms. It's just the two of us and the nighttime sounds of the hospital. The only light comes from the hallway. I've been shown how to get you to attach to my breast, but it's hard to do and you don't want to do it. You seem to be looking around for something else to latch on to. I'm starting to panic when the nurse comes back to check on us. She shows me again, and finally we get it. Your tiny pink hand wraps tightly around my finger.

In the morning, my parents come to pick us up. My mother pushes the wheelchair the hospital requires toward the big double exit doors. You're bundled snugly in a yellow blanket. I watch my father's back as he leads the way, walking three steps ahead. He's wearing a brown leather jacket. His pants are riding low on his skinny hips. "Wait here," he says to my mother.

We wait while he goes around to the parking lot to get the car. In the vestibule, between the two sets of doors, the cold wind blows in from outside. My mother rifles through her big bag, looking for a sweater, but can't find it.

"Don't worry about it, Ma," I tell her impatiently, thinking, I'll do better, Minnow. I'll always keep you warm.

We see my father's Buick pull up to the curb, and I stand, slowly. My mother follows with outstretched arms as if she thinks I might drop you. After ten minutes of trying to figure out how to use the newly purchased car seat, we get you strapped in, and I slide in beside you. My father pulls out into the stop-and-start of rush-hour traffic. As we crawl along, I can hear the sound of his worry. He takes a breath, holds it too long, and lets out a sigh. I feel a little queasy and think about how I used to get really carsick when I was a kid, but now, mostly, I don't anymore.

We arrive at my building and find a spot across the street.

I haven't told my parents about the mugging because I know they'd freak out, but I can't help but think about it as I give my dad the key and he holds the front door open. For a second, I clearly remember my mugger's angry face.

My mother brings her overnight bag inside. She's going to stay with us for a while.

At night, she crowds me to the edge of my narrow bed, but I'm thankful to have her there. You wake up hungry every hour. I'm so tired, it feels like I'm hallucinating or dreaming. "Sleep," she says, and I close my eyes under the warm blankets. I know it won't be long before you need to nurse again.

I listen to her change your diaper. She covers your belly with noisy kisses. She calls you butterball and sweetie pie.

After the first couple of days, we start to argue. She wants to do things her own way, and I want them done according to the books I've studied and my own good sense.

"There's nothing wrong with her. It's just gas," says my mother.

"Oh, baloney. I tested it on my wrist," she says.

"She's in pain, Mom," I tell her.

"It's too hot, Mom," I say.

I'm easily annoyed and she's always wrong. That's the way it feels.

The pressure of my irritation continues to increase, until one morning I go too far. I raise my voice and say something awful. "Just give her to me!" I say in exasperation. "Why can't you *ever* make things easier instead of harder?!"

There seems no way to take the awful thing back once it's said. I've hurt her feelings but I can't bring myself to say I'm sorry. For a whole day we look after you in silence, both feeling dreadful, until finally we resume talking, tentatively, carefully, and decide together that she should go home for now.

The days are a blur after she goes. I'm always sleeping and

waking, feeding you, changing your diaper, walking you in circles, singing to you, telling you everything is going to be all right. I go days without showering. I don't leave the apartment at all.

When my mother calls to check on us, I try not to take out my exhaustion on her, but she is often my involuntary target. I don't know why. Shouldn't having my own daughter cause me to be kinder to my mother? But my anger is irrational and quick, as if she's to blame for something.

My sister calls from Miami. I tell her our mother is driving me crazy, but she only wants to talk about you. She asks me to hold the phone up to your ear so you'll remember the sound of her voice. "I don't want her to forget me," she says.

I remember when she was a baby. I used to climb into her crib. I used to yell to my mother, "Ma! The baby's crying!"

Now you're the crying baby, Minnow. I pick you up and hold you. Usually you're just hungry, but sometimes it's a bad dream, or some other mysterious reason. You fit perfectly in the curve between my jaw and shoulder.

I sing you the songs my father sang to me when I was small. He had the sweetest voice. *I gave my love a cherry without a stone. I gave my love a chicken without a bone.*

Your crying wears us both out. I take you back to bed with me so we can sleep for an hour or two.

Twenty-seven

Jules sends an enormous fruit basket, wrapped in cellophane, with a tin of sugar cookies at its center. After I polish off the cookies, I live on the apples, oranges, and pears. My hunger makes it the most delicious fruit I've ever tasted. Then another big package arrives from her. Inside is an exquisite dress for you, Minnow, purchased at Harrods. Jules has been living in London, in Kensington or Chelsea, since her film wrapped, but the enclosed note says she'll see us soon. She's coming home to spend Christmas with her family.

When she arrives with a grocery bag full of Christmas dinner, I've got you in the dress. We greet her at the door, and she laughs out loud, the way she does. I can't argue when she says you aren't merely beautiful, but radiant and dripping in charisma. It's so good to have her company. I'm hungry for our talks. She decides we have to have a tree and goes out into the cold, alone. When she returns, she's got two young guys trailing behind her, carrying an enormous blue spruce between them.

The tree practically fills the room with its long branches and heavy scent. We drink hot tea and string popcorn, sit on the floor and dissect one another's problems until they've been cut up into nothing.

When Jules ducks outside to the garden for a smoke, I take a peek at you napping in the nursery and find you awake, resting peacefully. You look up at me with serious eyes. I pick you up and kiss your warm forehead. Through the window, I can see Jules, glamorous in her camel coat with the fox-fur collar.

When she comes back inside, rubbing her hands together to warm them, she takes you from my arms and tells you the story of how once we found out we had the same boyfriend. She calls him Bighead.

"Once upon a time, Minnow, there was a man named Bighead who loved your mommy and loved me, too, but your mommy and I loved each other more."

I think of the first time I ever saw Bighead, jogging along Central Park, on the cobblestone sidewalk of Fifth Avenue. I remember he glanced back over his shoulder, to give me a second look, and caught me slack-jawed, in awe. He was ridiculously handsome, a six-foot-four actor with thick, wavy hair and twinkling brown eyes.

"He played us the same song on his guitar," she says.

"It was the only one he knew," I add.

"And told us the exact same stories. But we laughed when we found out, and if it hurt our feelings, we let our friendship make us feel better, because that's what friends do for one another, little Minnow."

Jules's laugh is like a bell. After she leaves to catch her train, the apartment feels very quiet. I eat the turkey dinner she brought straight from the containers and sing all the Christmas songs I know: "Silent Night," "Come, All Ye Faithful," and the rest. The only Chanukah song I remember is the one about a dreidel, and I sing it to you, though it's not as pretty as the others.

I watch you try to stay awake. Your eyes drift closed and open again, but finally you give in to sleep.

There's no word from Gabriel. At first, I jump like Pavlov's dog when the phone rings. I figure someone is bound to tell him, and even if they don't, it must occur to him that you're here by now. But as the weeks go by, I begin to wonder if he'll ever call.

On the morning of New Year's Eve, I wake up feeling hopeful. All day I'm jumpy with anticipation. The phone rings and it's Jules, and then Alan. My sister calls from Miami. But there's no call from Gabriel.

In the original 1982, *I* call him. I leave a rambling message on his machine and he calls back from Caracas, where he's gone to play a New Year's show with Eddie's band. He has to shout to hear himself over the festivities. "What are you doing?"

"I'm on my way to a party," I say, shouting, too, though in fact I'm in my pajamas watching Dick Clark on TV. We speak for barely a minute before he says the fireworks are starting and he has to go. I hear a woman's voice and laughter and feel unbearably lonely. Then he's gone, and the year is gone, confetti falling, and Dick Clark saying good night.

This time, I don't even think about trying to call him and, though I miss him, I don't feel lonely. I roast a chicken for dinner and open a bottle of red wine, have only a single glass because I'm still nursing. I rock you in the red rocking chair, listening to Rickie Lee Jones sing "Company." She'll remember him too clearly. Her voice is like a sob.

In the last minutes before midnight, I wrap you in a blanket and take you out to the garden to look up at the stars. They're hard to see in New York City because of ambient light and clouds. But the night is crystal clear, and I locate one at the edge of Orion's belt. I point it out to you and make a wish. "Please let us run into him," I say out loud. The wish fills me with excitement as if it actually brings him closer. Then I kiss your soft cheek and we begin 1983 together, just the two of us, in our garden under that pale star.

Twenty-eight

There's a word for what happens when you stay indoors too long and start to feel you can't go out, the world is too intense:

agoraphobia. I think I have it. I order food in, have groceries and diapers delivered, run to the corner and back, with you in my arms, my coat thrown over my pajamas.

But finally one day I decide it's time. I bundle you up in a sweater, warm socks, and a hat. I tuck layers of blankets around you in your carriage, put on my heavy coat and gloves. Out into the world we go, north on Broadway to Seventy-second Street and east to Columbus Avenue. The sun is out and it's not too cold. The light is bouncing off every shiny surface, glittering the way it does in winter.

As we make our way past all the restaurants and bars on Columbus Avenue, I point out the landmarks, the corners where your father and I kissed, or fought, the bars we closed at four in the morning. I hardly notice all the passersby, but sometimes they break into our bubble. They look into the carriage and smile. They make unsolicited comments:

"She's so beautiful!"

"How old?"

"Congratulations!"

"So precious."

"Bless her heart."

I mumble thank you and return their smiles with lowered eyes. I seem to have lost the ability to engage in casual conversation. I wish I had sunglasses to hide behind because my eyes are tearing in the bright sunlight, and I don't want anyone to think I'm crying.

Soon we're crossing Seventy-seventh Street, and I see the green awning of the Café Miriam ahead. I'm excited to introduce you to my friends.

When I wheel you inside, Sofia is the first one I see. She's standing there with her hands on her hips. She's got a new hairstyle, kind of an asymmetric shag. She screams when she sees us, and reaches down into the carriage to pick you up. "What a little angel!" she says. You're tiny in her arms. I'm almost embarrassed by how beautiful you are. It feels like it might be a sin to be as proud as I am.

We take a deuce, a table for two, by the window. All the other girls come over to hold you, too. "Have you heard from him?" Nina asks.

"Nope," I say, and change the subject.

Sofia takes her order pad from her apron. She makes a face, says in a goofy voice, "What will it be?"

I've missed her, and the others, and even working at the restaurant. It feels strange to be there as a customer. When the man at the next table asks for a coffee refill, I want to jump up and get it for him. I'm aware of who needs a check and who hasn't gotten their entrée yet.

I watch as one waitress holds you and passes you to another. Will leans across the bar to touch your cheek. You're being so good, but finally you start to cry. I listen as they attempt to soothe you and force myself not to come to your rescue. When Vicky brings you back, I realize I've been holding my breath. As soon as you're in my arms, you stop crying.

Vicky sits down across from us. "You ready to come back to work?"

I tell her I think I'll be ready soon, though it's hard to imagine being ready.

"You can start off with a couple of shifts," she says. "Have you looked into child care?"

I've been hoping I might be able to bring you to work with me, but can see now that it's probably not very realistic. "I still need to figure that out," I say. I don't feel too worried yet. My parents are still helping with health insurance, and I've got some money left in the bank.

By the time my food gets to the table, I think you've had enough excitement. It's time to change your diaper and give you lunch. I ask to have the food wrapped up and say a quick good-bye to everyone.

"Hang on, Little One," I tell you, pushing the carriage home.

We're exhausted by the time we get back. I change your diaper and take you into my bed to nurse. When you've had your fill, we both fall asleep.

Twenty-nine

In March, I go back to work three nights a week. I put you in your pajamas, the pink ones with the kittens, or the yellow ones with feet, and take you upstairs to Maria's apartment with your blanket and your rabbit. You're eating some pureed foods now, and I've prepared a bottle. Maria is our neighbor on four. We met her in the basement laundry room. She said she did some babysitting, if we ever needed help. Maria is a grandmother. She speaks to you in Spanish. She gives you your supper and lets you watch TV until you fall asleep.

When I pick you up just before midnight, after my shift, you're out cold. Maria hands you to me in the doorway, because her husband, Hector, is sleeping. He has to get up at four in the morning. I pay her in cash, eight dollars an hour. It's a little more than half of what I make.

We whisper so quietly it's like lipreading.

"Good night, Maria. Thank you so much."

"No problem. Such a good baby."

All night I've longed for this moment, to smell your baby

sweetness and feel your astoundingly soft skin against mine. I carry you downstairs and into the nursery without turning on the light. The moon is shining in the window, and the only noise is the distant rush of traffic on Broadway. As I lay you down in your crib, my heart feels big, like it's pushing out against my rib cage. I watch you sleep for a long time. Your tiny chest rises and falls. Finally, I walk the few steps to my own bed and fall into it without even washing off my makeup or brushing my teeth.

At work, I miss you and worry that you're missing me. I tell the girls about all the funny things you do. You have a great sense of humor and laugh at any silly game I come up with. You're smart, too. I can see your brain working, trying to figure things out. You want to touch everything in your reach.

You look like Gabriel and like me. You have his perfectly shaped lips and intelligent eyes, my coloring and stubborn chin, our broad cheekbones and heavy eyelids. You had Gabriel's balding pate, too, which worried me a little, but finally your hair has started coming in soft, light brown waves. It curls around your slightly pointy ears and at the back of your delicate neck. You have blond highlights, too, like the ones women pay hundreds of dollars for on Madison Avenue.

I realize, looking at you, that Gabriel and I could be brother and sister, our resemblance is so strong. Before you were born, it never occurred to me. Now you remind me of it every day.

I hear rumors about Gabriel. He's going to make a movie. He's collaborating with famous rock artists. I listen to the stories with one ear but try not to dwell on them.

The only one that really gets my attention is when I hear his wife has had a miscarriage. They say she can't have any more children. I have no idea if it's true, but I feel deeply sorry when I hear it. I suppose that might seem strange to you, Minnow, but I wouldn't wish it on anyone.

In the original 1983, when I hear about their lost baby, my eyes fill instantly. An ache spreads through me, heavy as a bag of sand. I know what it is to lose someone never touched, or kissed, or held.

Thirty

We visit Jules at her new apartment in the West Village. It has a whole wall of exposed brick and windows that overlook a little park. The floor tiles in the kitchen are stylishly black and white. We watch as she grinds whole beans and makes strong black coffee in a French press.

Jules is flush with movie money and speaks of her luxuries and privileges as if they are commonplace. But she's generous with you, so I try not to feel like a poor relation. You're the best-dressed daughter of a struggling waitress, ever. She's taken us to FAO Schwarz and bought you enormous bears and blue-eyed baby dolls. Your nursery overflows with a jungle of stuffed animals and other toys.

She holds you, rocks her leg, wags her foot. She's dying for a cigarette. The constant motion puts you to sleep.

Conspiracy, Jules's big movie, is scheduled to open soon, and she is overwhelmed with publicity commitments. She has offers for other movies but has rejected one for the nudity the role requires, and another because she'd be little more than arm candy. She's going to hold out for the good parts, although

her manager and agent tell her those are few and far between.
They're encouraging her to work as much as she can, to strike
while the iron is hot, but Jules dismisses their advice. She believes things will always be as they are.

This is how it is when you're young, Minnow. You have no
sense of the temporary nature of opportunity, the temporary
nature of everything, in fact. You think it's all going to last
forever.

Jules talks about her time in London, her dinners with
movie stars, her interviews and auditions. Hearing about it all
makes me feel that I am missing my chance, that life is passing me by. I want to be out there in the world, too. I want to
prove something to my family, to show my father he's wrong
about me. I want to have a big life like Jules and Gabriel.

But then you begin to cry and she hands you back to me.
Your sweet baby scent is like a balm. The rush of love I feel
reminds me of what's important.

The premiere for *Conspiracy* is on a Tuesday night. I'm on
the schedule to work Tuesdays, but swap with Sofia. Jules is
going early to do interviews. She says she'll leave my name on
a guest list at the door and that I should meet her inside.

I'd love to buy something new to wear, but even if I had the
money I wouldn't know what to buy. On the day of the premiere, I put you in your carriage and we take the subway downtown to a thrift store on East Fifth Street. I've gotten the hang
of it now, carrying you in the stroller down the steep stairs.
Sometimes someone offers to help, but they hold their end at the
wrong angle or move too quickly. It's easier just to do it myself.

At the thrift store, the clothing is piled up so high you can
see it mashed up against the front window from the street.
I've been coming here for years. You have to plow through the
piles. It's a treasure hunt. In the fifteen-dollar pile, I find a

black velvet dress with spaghetti straps and little velvet balls that hang from the top of the bodice. I think it's from the sixties. It's lined in satin, not like the cheap stretchy velvet you get now. I hold it up against me. It looks about right.

"That's a cool dress," the punk girl behind the counter says.

I look over at you, bundled up in your carriage, stationary as a sack of flour. I pay for the dress, and the girl hands it back to me in a plain plastic bag. I hope it fits. Most of my baby weight has gone, but I'm not the skinny girl I used to be. At the last minute I decide to dye my hair, too, and pick up a box of Clairol Medium Summer Blonde at the drugstore.

The dress is a total score. It's tight up and down. I just hope the zipper holds because I'm bursting out of it, and it's an old zipper.

The hair dyeing is less successful. I don't spend much time reading the directions, because you're getting fussy and need to eat and have a nap before I leave you with Maria. My hair looks sort of blond in the darkish light of my living room, but in the bathroom, I can clearly see it's green, and not a good green. I'm not sure what I've done wrong, but it's too late to do anything about it now. I put on my makeup with one hand, holding on to you with the other. You keep reaching for my mascara wand and then my lipstick. Minnow, you really make me laugh.

At about seven-thirty, I grab your diaper bag and your rabbit, your bottle, and a jar of carrots, and rush up the stairs to leave you with Maria.

I hand her the bag and the bottle and the rabbit. But I'm slow to let you go. "She ate twenty minutes ago, and I just changed her diaper."

"*Dame la niña,*" she says to me, her fingers wagging, and then to you, "Come here, *mi gordita.*"

There's a part of me that regrets handing you over every time. Maria sees it in my face. "Go have fun, Lisa. We'll be just fine. Wave bye-bye to your mama." She takes your little hand and waves it around. You look up into her face. "Good night, Mommy," she says, and takes you inside.

I make my way carefully down the three flights of stairs, in my high heels, to the street. I'm wearing a shabby coat over the velvet dress, but a man goes by and gives me a long whistle, and I almost forget my hair is green.

On the corner I hail a taxi. "Sixtieth and Second," I tell the driver. He's got cool jazz playing on the radio. I look out the window as we fly across town. New York City has the best people watching in the world. You see couples in love, men in hats, women hurrying with shopping bags, all the different coats, boots, hairstyles, people of every color, age, and shape.

It's almost spring again. Only a year ago, I walked the streets of the Upper West Side, excited and nervous, wondering what you'd be like. I can almost see myself walk by. I was another person a year ago. I think of your father and feel deeply sad. I still miss him. It never becomes less. When I catch my reflection in the glass, I note again that I've become someone whose resting face falls into a mournful expression.

As if the cabdriver can read my thoughts, he says, "Smile! It can't be that bad."

This is one you hear a lot as a young woman, Minnow. Why do men think we enjoy being commanded to smile? I meet his eyes in the rearview mirror, but don't give him what he wants.

As we pull up to the theater, I see Jules standing on the red carpet in a long black dress. She's lifting her chin and posing for the cameras. She's as lovely as Grace Kelly. Walking past her, I feel a combination of two things: unbearable pride and uncomfortable envy. She sneaks a look at me over her shoulder and gives me her real smile, the one that says, *Can you believe this craziness?* I give her one back. The photographers jump to see who I am. I hope I don't have lipstick on my teeth.

But they lose interest quickly. "She isn't anybody," I hear one say.

The movie is a complicated thriller involving the Israeli secret police, Russian spies, and the CIA. The plot is so confusing, I lose track of who is who. Jules plays two characters. She is a freedom fighter and a woman in a young lieutenant's dream. As a soldier, her hair is shorn, her brow furrowed. She appears suddenly in a doorway. Then she's running down the hall. As the dream girl, she wears a sheer white gown. Her platinum-blond wig falls over her face. When she tilts her head, the long wig parts like a curtain to reveal red painted lips.

After the screening, I pile into a car with Jules and her publicist to go to the after-party at a nearby hotel. She is whisked away as soon as we arrive. I stand in line to get something to eat at the buffet and sit at a table by myself. Everyone at the party seems ambitious and fake to me. I watch them walk around the room, trying to gauge whether conversation with one person or another is worth their time. I don't talk to anyone, and no one talks to me. What a shallow world, I think, feeling self-conscious about my green hair. Even the velvet dress suddenly feels like a shabby rag. I think of you waiting for me at Maria's and just want to go home.

When I find Jules to tell her I'm leaving, she holds her hand up to her ear like a phone and mouths, "I'll call you." But she's so busy that she forgets to call. Or maybe she's waiting for me to call her, but I don't call either.

It happens pretty much the same way in the original 1983. *Conspiracy* makes Jules a movie star. She rents a house on the West Coast and has all her belongings shipped out there. We don't get to see her again for a very long time.

Thirty-one

In the morning, Maria comes downstairs. I fix her a cup of tea and we sit in the garden wearing our coats. It's almost May but there's still frost on the ground. Maria's hair is the most incredible shade of silver. When she glances in the mirror to smooth the ends, she sucks her cheeks in ever so slightly. You seem to think she's perfect in every way.

She's teaching you to speak Spanish and points to the illustrations in your books. "Dog: *el perro.* Cat: *el gato.*"

I know a few words and phrases that Gabriel once taught me, but I never became fluent. I was like his parrot. He'd teach me to say something funny and I'd repeat it. Then he'd laugh. I still love to speak the few words I remember, but I don't have a natural talent for other languages. Maybe you will.

"House: *la casa.* Grandmother: *la abuela.*"

You make lots of sounds but nothing is quite Spanish, or even English. "Ba, ba, ga, ga," you say, and laugh.

We laugh with you.

Maria teaches me things, too. She shows me how to wash the floors with white wine vinegar. She tells me the best kind of paper towels to buy. She gives me a special soap for washing baby things and underwear. She talks about cleaning as if it is both an art and a feature of good character. Her highest compliment is: "Now, *she* knows how to clean."

Maria has a son and she used to have a daughter. The girl died of cancer a long time ago in a city called La Rioja, in Argentina. That's where Maria grew up, married Hector, and raised her children. "Now it is only boys," she says, referring to her son and his sons.

Though Maria is nothing like my mother, there is something of mother and daughter in the bond we forge. It seems easier to accept mothering from her because she is *not* my mother. I know that doesn't make sense.

I look at you, Minnow, and feel how much it would hurt to have you replace me with a capable woman from Argentina. I make it a point to call my mother just before bedtime. "Listen to this, Ma," I say, and hold the phone up to your mouth. "Minnow, say good night to your *abuela*."

Thirty-two

It's summer again before we run into Gabriel. We're on Hudson, coming from a shop in the West Village, when I see him on Bank Street, heading right toward us. It takes him a moment to recognize me. He does a double take, which hurts a little, because I'd know him anywhere, instantly. But then he sees us and looks genuinely shocked and happy. His face crumples and his eyes light up.

I've got you strapped to my chest in a baby harness. So when he throws his arms around me, you're squashed between us and I think it's one of the finest moments of my life. I know how an astronaut feels reentering the earth's atmosphere, the relief of a deep-sea diver breaking through to the surface for oxygen. It's a please-God-stop-time moment, for sure, and I breathe him in long and deep. But then he lets me go, and I can see there is a new distance between us.

"Gabriel, this is Minnow," I say. I can feel my heart pounding and my cheeks burning. You, on the other hand, are one cool customer, Minnow. You look up at him with your intelligent brown eyes as if you could take him or leave him. I'm not sure what it is I see in his expression as he looks at your face. Is it awe? Is he afraid?

"Hi, Minnow," he says. His voice comes out half an octave too high. "She looks just like you."

"I think she looks like you."

We walk together, the three of us. There's a Mister Softee truck parked on the corner of Jane Street.

"Does she like ice cream?" Gabriel asks.

I'm usually careful about giving you sugar, but today is a special occasion. "Sure," I say.

"What flavor?"

"Better make it vanilla."

"How about you?"

"I'll have some of hers."

He gets himself a chocolate.

Hudson turns into Eighth Avenue and we continue to walk uptown. A man, a woman, a baby, and two ice cream cones. Anyone would take us for a family.

Gabriel tells me he's in town to finish packing up his things. The apartment at the Sheridan has been sold. It's the end of an era. For the rest of my life, I'll look up into that third-floor window when I go by and remember what it felt like to be inside looking out.

We walk and we talk. He doesn't mention his wife or ask anything about you. He says he's planning to return to his country soon. It's just a matter of time now. "Everyone is going to be very surprised," he says.

He'll never go back, I think to myself.

He adjusts the brim of his hat. I can see him making eye contact with every woman we pass. We walk through Chelsea and the desolate West Thirties, past a truck yard, the post office, and Penn Station. You crane your neck around to look at everything. You practice "ma-ma" and "ga-ga." You rest your head against my chest and fall asleep.

At about Forty-second Street, he seems to remember you. "Is she heavy?"

"A little. Want to carry her for a while?"

"Maybe we should take a cab."

"No, that's okay." I don't want it to be over. "I'm used to carrying her."

"Okay," he says.

So we walk through the theater district and the West Fifties, Columbus Circle, and Lincoln Center. The harness spreads your weight across my back, but by the time we reach West Seventy-first Street, I'm feeling every ounce of your eighteen pounds. My shoulders ache and my neck is sore. I'm tired and need to change your diaper, feed you, and put you down for a nap. I'm thinking that as soon as I let you down you're going to try to scramble across the floor. You've just started to crawl and need to be watched every second.

But I know what Gabriel is thinking. He's wondering whether or not there's a chance we might have sex.

I still want to, God help me. What kind of a man shows so little interest in his own daughter? I should be angry. I know that.

Still I ask him, "Do you want to come inside for a minute?"

Gabriel gives me the look: the up-and-down eyebrows, the lascivious smile, and I feel that tug in my belly that shuts off the part of my brain that knows better.

As soon as we're inside, he tries to pull me down on the bed. I've still got you strapped to me and start to panic. *"Wait!"* I say sharply.

He gives me a moment to free you, and as I undo the harness, I look into your beautiful, tired face and know that I can't. I don't want to. I mean I do want to. I want to pretty badly, but not more than I want to take care of you, my love. "I can't do this," I tell him. I've got you halfway to your changing table. I pick up a diaper from the shelf.

"Sure you can, baby." He's right behind me. He's kissing my neck and undoing my bra.

But I push him off. "Stop it!" My breasts are full of milk. You're hungry, and I've had enough of Gabriel for the moment.

He stands in the doorway and waits while I change you. He continues to wait while I sit with you in the red rocking chair and guide your mouth to my breast. As you nurse, you reach up with one hand to hold a piece of my hair. I look over at him standing there, still waiting.

"Are you sure?" he asks me.

"Yes, I'm sure." *Go, please just go.*

As soon as he leaves, the tears come. Not because I regret my decision. I promise you, Minnow, I do not. But I wish things were different, and that wish is painful.

Thirty-three

Alan sounds guilty or sorry. I can hear it in his voice in the first instant. He's called to tell me he's going on tour with Charlotte Winter. Charlotte's a singer-songwriter whose music is not really like mine, but since we're both young women who play the guitar, it's likely the music business would put us in the same category. In the past, Alan and I have talked about Charlotte, the fact that she's pretty good but not as good as I am. We've wondered whether her success was using up my chance or paving the way for it. Now it's a moot point, because I'm not going anywhere, and Alan needs the gig.

He comes over. He's got a meatball hero with him in a greasy bag. "Hungry?"

I am. We tear into it.

Minnow, you're bouncing up and down on a swing suspended in the bedroom doorway. You've got the best temperament and are content just to bounce and look around. You reach for the cats as they brush by you.

"She's been watching *Sesame Street,* and I swear she's already learning her numbers and letters," I tell Alan.

"She's the cutest," he says, but he seems distracted.

"You don't have to feel bad," I say. "I'll see you when you get back. I'll have ten new songs written by then." Alan's the kind of person who feels bad when there's no reason to. He can't help it. He feels he's betraying me. Sure, I'm jealous not to be the one going on tour, but I'm glad for him. I'm proud of him. He's beat out other guitar players to get this gig. These are important years for establishing relationships. You end up working with many of the same people for your entire career.

For a sideman like Alan, it's especially important to make the connections.

"Are you sure you're okay with this?" he asks me again.

"Yes! I am one hundred percent okay!"

After he goes, I pick up the guitar and play "Still True." You sort of sing along and it makes me laugh. I really am okay.

In the original 1983, my heart aches to love someone the way I love you. I try to soothe it with music, but music isn't enough. I try loving a man with my whole being, but romantic love is so limited. I think it's only meant to get you to the next phase. I get stuck on it like a record that skips.

Thirty-four

Just when I think I can't take another minute at the restaurant, another job presents itself. This is how it happens: I'm standing over a famous record producer, coffeepot in hand, when I hear him say that a recording studio on East Thirteenth Street called Silver Sound is looking for a receptionist. He's holding his cup in the air and doesn't even look at me as I fill it. But I call the studio as soon as I get home and drop his name.

In my interview, I'm not sure how I do it, but I become the perfect candidate for the job. I'm a good liar, or maybe I'm able to convince myself that yes, I've been a receptionist before (I've answered the phone, haven't I?) and no, it shouldn't be any problem if sometimes I need to be there all night. Harv, the owner of the studio, tells me he's got a couple more people to interview and he'll get back to me, but I have a feeling I've got the job, and by the time I get home there's a message on my answering machine asking if I can come in the following day at noon. I haven't mentioned anything about bringing my baby to work, but when I come in the next day with you and all your things, Harv seems to be okay with it. I set up your portable playpen next to my desk. Every time Harv passes by, I give him a smile and a wave. I tell you, Minnow, pretty girls get away with murder.

Not that I don't do a good job, because I do. I come in at half-past eleven, get you set up, and make a fresh pot of coffee. It's a rare session that starts before noon. I answer the phones and order lunch for everybody. It's fun meeting all the working musicians, the producers and engineers. I learn a lot about recording, too.

The only drag about the job is the studio is as dark as a cave. All the windows are in a hallway that faces an alley. But I make sure you get to feel the sunshine and breathe real air. We get up early. We have our breakfast and go to the playground. By the time we get to Silver Sound, it's almost time for your nap. You have your lunch and I lay you down with your rabbit and your blanket. You sleep so soundly, nothing disturbs you, not the guys getting drum sounds in room A, not even the wail of electric guitar coming from C.

After your nap, you're only grumpy for a few minutes before you get happy and want to know what's going on. You're unbelievable, talking your made-up language, walking your drunken walk down the hall. You have to say hello to everybody. You're a miniature Gabriel. Charming everybody is what you do naturally. All you need is a wide-brimmed hat and a pair of maracas.

One day I hear that Corbin won't be coming in and note a slight feeling of disappointment. This is the beginning of my crush. I haven't been with a man since before you were born, and I'm certainly not on the lookout for anybody, but it occurs to me it might be nice to have someone to have fun with, to hang out with. Of course, he can't be just anybody. He's got to give me that twist in my belly. He has to make me laugh. Corbin does both of those things. He's tall and thin with bright dark eyes and eyelashes so long they rest on his cheek when he looks down. He wears skinny black Levi's and washed-out T-shirts with the faded names of rock bands. He's kind of dorky and cool at the same time. I hear somebody say he's from Austin, Texas.

When a producer doesn't bring his own engineer, or a band books time without one, they use Corbin, or Don, who is nowhere near as cute. Both guys work for the studio, like me. They do equipment repairs and talk endlessly about pro audio gear. But Corbin has another side, too. The first thing I ever noticed about him was his beautiful handwriting. He labels the boxes of two-inch tape with a thick black marker in a style that is artistic, yet tidy. I guess it's weird to find someone's handwriting so appealing, but I do.

Of course, the eyelashes don't hurt either.

I think Corbin falls for you first, Minnow. He's always coming up with nicknames for you. He calls you Speedy, Tumbleweed, Jellybean, Peanut.

The thing between us develops slowly. We become friends first. Corbin is a few years younger than I am. He's just out of school. He seems like a baby compared to Gabriel, but maybe that's why he feels safe to me. Even though he's really smart, I feel I know more about life.

The first time we kiss, it's two in the morning and you're fast asleep. It's just us at the studio. We're in room A, the big room. I'm playing my songs for him and he's listening so quietly I look up to make sure he's still there.

"You're really good," he says. His lips are purple from the wine we're drinking.

It's pride or gratefulness that makes me lean in to kiss his fuzzy cheek. He pulls me to him, kisses me on the mouth, and I get that delicious first-kiss rush. His lips are soft. His scent, a kind of earthy-sweet-boy smell, fills my nostrils. I notice he has smile lines at the outer edges of his eyes and try to remember if I own even one decent pair of underwear.

Corbin jumps up to set up a microphone in the middle of the room. He grabs a pair of headphones off the wall. "Play it again, just like that," he says, putting the phones over my head. I watch his skinny back as he bounds into the control room, and then he's behind the glass, pushing buttons and moving faders on the board. "Sing a little," he says through the intercom.

We start recording like that, in the middle of the night, whenever somebody else's session gets canceled or ends early. Sometimes we have a drummer and bass player come down. I learn how to use a microphone, to sing softly into it when I'm up close and pull back when I want to sing out.

If life with Gabriel was swimming in the ocean, then being with Corbin is splashing around in a kids' pool. We're silly together, playful as puppies. We arm-wrestle and tickle each other. We make up funny names for everything. There's a lightness to it I've never known.

One February day the whole city closes down after a big snowstorm, and we three go sledding in Central Park. You're about fifteen months by then, Minnow. Oh, how you love the snow. We hike into the park, me pulling the sled, and you up on Corbin's shoulders. All around us children and their parents are doing the same. We find a good hill and pile onto the Flexible Flyer. You laugh your head off going down the slope. Fearless girl. You giggle and squeal. You lean back into me as we gather speed, and as soon as we get to the bottom, you say: "More!"

Corbin teases you, playfully, and you laugh. You hide behind my leg and jump out to surprise him. You shout, "No, Bin," which is what you call him.

"Bin is so silly," I say, smiling at the two of you.

We climb back up the hill and go down again and again. After what must be a dozen times or more, I stagger over to a stand of trees and lie flat on my back.

"Mama!" you shout. You scamper down next to me and I take you in my arms. We play the game where I try to kiss your face and you pretend you want me to stop. Above us, the tall trees look dramatic and magical. Every dark branch is covered with ten inches of undisturbed snow. Beyond them, I can see the rooflines of all the majestic buildings on Central Park West.

You climb on top of me like a little monkey. You pull my hair and tug at my face.

"Minnow, stop." I laugh, which only makes you do it more.

How many days like this before I began to take one for granted? The way people with a constant view of purple mountains come to scarcely notice them. I know what it is to walk alone past the screams and laughter of children and their families playing in the snow. The thought brings tears of gratitude to my eyes.

"Anybody interested in a hot chocolate?" Corbin's silhouette stands between us and the afternoon sun.

"Sure," I say. I stand and pull you to your feet, brush the

snow from your back. Corbin hoists you over his head and onto his shoulders. I trail behind, pulling the sled, wiping my wet eyes with a soggy mitten.

"Ooh, stinky," I hear him say. "I think somebody needs a diaper change."

Thirty-five

Now that you're more mobile, Minnow, sometimes we take the bus. It's not that I mind the subway—it's the fastest and cheapest way to get around town—but sometimes I don't feel like going underground. On the bus, you're riding above the traffic, past pedestrians and the mad activity of the city. It takes a while to get where you're going. A kind of intimacy develops between all the passengers.

One day, I find I'm looking at everyone on the bus and imagining each person as a baby. All these freaky people, stressed out and anxious, pale, frowning, and buried in layers of old coats and scratchy-looking wool hats. Every one of them was once someone's baby.

There I am, with you on my lap. Still, what I think about is: Why does the world need so many babies, so many people? Clearly, everyone feels the need to reproduce, but does that mean everybody should?

I start to get really worked up thinking about how selfish it is. How many people have children just because they don't know what else to do with their lives, or because they think they're supposed to, or because they're terrified to be alone? We're a species with a population problem!

Just then, I notice your shoe is missing. It's fallen off some-where. Your pink sock is about to slip off, too. I give it a tug and get up to look around. Perhaps the shoe has come off on the bus.

One of the former babies, an old man in a brown overcoat, finds it in the aisle. He's a little bent with scoliosis and holds on to the seat backs as he makes his way to us. He smiles warmly as he hands the shoe to me. I thank him, and he says, "My pleasure, young lady."

I notice a lot of the other passengers are looking and smil-ing, too. I feel sorry then, for wishing them never born. There is kindness radiating from their faces.

There may be no greater human quality than kindness, Minnow. This is a revelation I come to as an older woman, and there's no way I would have known it that day on the bus. But I need to fill the girl I was with lessons learned by the woman I became. I need to give her perspective, to ground her, so when she gets off that bus with you in her arms and turns to wave at her fellow passengers, who are waving back through the dark windows, she can be uplifted by the exchange. I need her to be healed by such things so that she can be a good mother to you and make the most of this second chance for both of us.

Thirty-six

Corbin moves into the apartment on West Seventy-first Street. He builds himself a rustic cupboard to hold his things. The place is small for the three of us, but he turns the yard into his workshop. He makes shelves and benches, and even a little chair for you. He labels boxes of baby things with their contents, cleans out the medicine chest and the refrigerator. He paints the kitchen wall with chalkboard paint so we can write notes to one another. Little by little, he brings a Corbin kind of order to our lives.

He's a natural with you, too, Minnow, maybe because he's really a kid himself. He tells you silly jokes and never tires of coming up with games for you to play. He hangs a swing for you in the yard, and I have to tell him not to push you so high.

When I see you're getting attached to him, it warms my heart, but it also worries me, because although I don't want to be thinking about Gabriel, I see him in your face every day. A part of me is still waiting for him. I know it isn't rational, but hope lives in me like a stubborn amnesiac. It causes me to pull back from Corbin sometimes. I never say a word about Gabriel, but he can feel me slip away. He tells me my eyes have gone cold. "Where'd ya go?" he asks suspiciously.

Sometimes we argue, and he storms off and doesn't come back until the next day. When he gets home I say, "We can't do that in front of her, Corbin. I mean it. I won't have her growing up around people screaming and slamming doors."

"Well, maybe you need to figure out what you want," he growls petulantly.

He holds the music over my head when he's angry. He has control of my recordings. We've added cello and trumpet. A percussionist has laid down some hand drums and tambourine. Layers of electric guitars, keyboards, piano, and background vocals add momentum to the choruses. The closer the songs get to being completed, the larger his threat. He could take the tapes. He could destroy them.

Still, when things are going well between us, I allow myself to imagine a future with Corbin. I can picture us sitting around the long table with a house full of kids. We could grow our own brood. I could play music and he could make furniture. Maybe we could be happy.

Corbin is jealous of Alan at first, too. But it doesn't take long before they become friends. They share a love of electronics, musical instruments, and techie stuff. They can talk for hours about some latest guitar pedal or gadget.

Alan gets in the habit of coming by on Sunday afternoons when he's in town. There's usually a game on TV that nobody watches. They talk and Alan keeps an eye on whatever's in the oven while I play with you on the floor.

You have little interest in your toy piano, or the dolls that I once loved. You only want to put puzzles together or play with LEGO's Fabuland. There are hundreds of plastic pieces around us in primary-colored piles.

"Aren't you afraid she going to choke on that?" Alan asks.

"She loves to build. I can't stop her. Watch."

I take a red LEGO piece from your hand, and you scrunch up your eyes and open your mouth to wail: "Mama!"

"See?"

"Leave the kid alone," Corbin says.

I hand it back to you and instantly you resume building.

"Is that a firehouse, Minnow?"

"Fi-ouse," you say.

When I try to help you, you push my hand away. So I build my own structures beside you. You watch me out of the corner of your eye, and think nothing of taking a desirable piece from my hand to add to your own construction. Together we build a LEGO town of buildings and bridges. When you get tired of the game, you stand up carefully on chubby legs and knock it all down.

"Nice work, Minnow," I say, laughing.

"No, Mama," you say sternly. These are your two favorite words.

I set the table and we sit down to eat, you in your high chair.

"How's Charlotte's new record doing?" I ask, sailing the spoon through the air like a plane. You make me work for each mouthful. Soon you'll begin terrible twos.

"She's getting great press," Alan says. "It's just a matter of time before she really hits."

I understand Corbin's jealousy then, because I feel sick with it myself.

"Who else is in the band?" Corbin asks.

Alan goes through the names and I can hear his pride and affection for everyone. He's as loyal as a dog, I think. But how can I resent it, when I know his greatest loyalty is to me?

After dinner, I put you to bed and we sit in the garden and play music. It takes him a minute to remember how my songs go. "How's your recording coming along?" he asks.

"We're almost done," Corbin says. "You should come down and add some finishing touches."

"Love to," Alan says, and I know he means it. But he's about to leave again, to go on the road with Charlotte. They'll be in Europe for the next month and a half, and we'll probably be finished before he gets back.

Thirty-seven

"Minnow is very smart," Maria says. We're on the way to my parents' house, the three of us, taking the train out to Long

Island for your birthday party. Corbin has to work. You're turning two this week, and my mother has invited everyone to celebrate.

"Her teacher says she is smarter than the other children," Maria continues. "She's good at language and math." Twice a week, in the mornings, you go to a preschool in the neighborhood. Maria picks you up on those days.

Now she holds you in her lap. You look out the window of the train as everything speeds by.

"Ca," you say.

"Car," I repeat.

"Bud."

"Bird."

"Whas'tha, Mama?"

"That's another train like this one," I tell you. "Train."

"Tain," you repeat.

My sister will be at the party. Lynn is being relocated to New York by her company. She's staying with my parents while she looks for a place to live.

At the station, my father's Buick is parked across the street. I hold the front door open for Maria, but she prefers to sit in the back. With my father's help, she gets you into the car seat, one, two, three.

"How was your ride?" my father asks as we drive the few blocks to their house.

"Fine," I say. "Maria was just telling me that the preschool thinks Minnow is smarter than the other two-year-olds."

"Of course she is," my father says, "but isn't she a little young to be in school?"

"It's only a couple of hours a week, Dad, and she likes going. It's good for her to socialize."

My father doesn't choose to respond to this. We pull into

the driveway. "Here we are," he says. Maria and I free you
from the car seat, and we go inside.

"There she is!" my mother says happily, in her singsong.
"Hello, Maria. How are you?" She takes our coats and hangs
them in the hall closet.

Maria finds a seat on the edge of the couch in the living
room. She's quieter than when it's just us.

My mother takes you from my arms and walks with you
past a stack of brightly wrapped presents on the hall table, and
into the kitchen to show you the cake she's baked. It has your
name written on it in pink icing.

"Mine," you say.

"That's right." Your grandmother laughs. "Later, we'll sing
'Happy Birthday' to you, and you can blow out the candles!"

"Where's Lynn?" I ask, and my mother tells me that my
sister is house hunting with our cousin Rachel.

"You remember Rachel is in real estate now," she says. It's
the first I've heard of it.

"Aunt Lou coming?" I ask. My mother says she expects her
older sister any minute. Aunt Lou lives just two towns away.

We return to the living room with paper and crayons to sit
on the floor and draw. My mother's drawing of a house and
trees is not bad.

"That's nice, Mom," I say.

"You thought you were the only artist in the family?" she
asks lightly.

As you draw, you begin to sing, softly at first, and then
louder. Your pitch is good, your voice high and clear. It doesn't
take much to encourage you to go through the whole reper-
toire. " 'Twinkle, Twinkle'?" I prompt.

Your version is one line long. You lift your feet to your hands
as you sing it and wiggle your toes.

" 'ABCs'?"

We laugh because you skip the lines you don't know and approximate the ones you do, blurring the consonants and connecting the vowels. We laugh with you and at you, too. We love you so much, Minnow.

Aunt Lou comes through the door. "Where is everybody?" she says.

"We're in here!" my mother calls.

My sister and cousin return chattering about the places they've seen.

You bounce between all the grown-ups, telling incomprehensible stories. My father lets you tug on his glasses. He speaks to you in a silly voice. Over your head, he watches the game.

In the following years, Lynn and Rachel will marry and have children and you'll be rich with young cousins, but today you are the only child and we watch you, exotic, rare, perfect girl, running, singing, talking, blowing out your birthday candles. "Happy birthday, dear Minnow! Happy birthday to you," we sing. You laugh and sing along, reflecting our love back to us.

Later, talking with my cousin at the kitchen table, I listen to her wonder aloud about the way fathers get to walk away without consequence. "Aren't we the ones who create this culture of privilege among men?" she asks. "Aren't we the ones who condone actions of irresponsibility amongst fathers?"

But how do you make a man behave the way you think he should?

"With laws that demand accountability," Rachel says.

I don't know. If he doesn't want to be in your life, do you really want to force him to be? I'd rather be alone, Minnow. There are plenty of worse fates.

Thirty-eight

Still, I have bills to pay and the money I make doesn't go very far. Not when it has to cover preschool, and babysitting, and shoes you grow out of every month. Maria returns a five out of the money I pay her. "Get something for yourself," she says, but I never do.

When I get up the nerve to ask Harv for a raise, he says he can't right now. Things are tight at the studio. He might even have to let one of the engineers go, he says, which means Corbin could soon be out of work. When I tell Corbin this, he shrugs his shoulders. He's not a worrier, which leaves the worrying to me.

At least my recording is done. When I can afford to, I plan to have cassette copies made of the best five songs and send them out to music attorneys and managers. But that seems like a faraway plan. We live on rice and beans and ramen noodles. We drink our coffee black. We fight because Corbin spends his money on beer.

All this time, I've kept Lois's dog-eared card in my underwear drawer, and one warm spring day I give her a call. We make a plan to meet for coffee at a place off Columbus Avenue called Cafe La Fortuna.

In the back garden, I see her sitting in a corner beneath one of the yellow umbrellas and give a little wave.

"Hi, Lisa," she says, standing and kissing me first on one cheek and then the other, European style. I do the same. Couple of Long Island girls, playing at sophistication.

I ask her what she's been up to, and I can tell by the way she answers that she isn't really dancing anymore. That's what happens. Dancers age out. It must be brutal for Lois, but she doesn't let on.

"How's your baby? You had a girl, right?" I can tell she knows I want something but she can't figure out what.

"Yes. She's going on three."

"Wow. Time flies."

"I know." I tell her about working at the studio, and how it doesn't pay much. I tell her I'm looking to make some extra money.

"What about the deadbeat dad?" she asks.

"Not in the picture," I say.

"And you don't want to go after him?"

"No, I don't."

She lifts a tiny cup of espresso to her lips, holding out her pinkie. She keeps her green eyes on mine. "Well, I know how you can make some money, but I don't think you're going to like it."

"Try me," I say.

She tells me about the massage parlor on lower Broadway where she's worked for about a year.

"The only problem is, I don't really know how to give a massage," I say.

She looks at me like I'm a dope, like I couldn't possibly be so innocent, but it's a genuine question. I know what she's talking about. I just don't know if I can fake the massage part. The rest I figure I can manage.

"They don't care about that," she says. "You just have to look pretty and be nice."

"I can be nice," I say.

She laughs a dry laugh. "Yeah, well, it's not as easy as you think."

And she's right.

I go in for an interview and am shown around the place. It's divided into eight little rooms, separated by thin, temporary walls. The rooms are only a little bigger than the massage tables in them. A single green plant sits on an empty desk in the reception area.

I'm told that the men pay in advance for the massage and any extras. They undress and cover themselves with a rough towel that smells of bleach. I make it clear that I don't want to be touched. I'll do the happy ending, but that's it.

It's a couple of weeks before I actually get up the nerve to take a shift at the massage parlor. I only have one day off a week from Silver, and it's hard to get away.

I've left Corbin to look after you; told him I was getting together with Lois and some other friends from the restaurant. I plan to be home in time to make dinner.

I'm a little nervous as I enter the tiny room. It feels too close. The man on the table is middle-aged. His reddish-blond hair could use a trim. I pull the towel back to his waist and put a little oil on his upper back. He lifts his head to look up at me, over his shoulder, and I recognize him. Damn. He's my old neighbor from East Seventy-eighth Street, the rich guy who lived in the house next door.

For a second, I see the recognition in his eyes. Then we pretend to be strangers. "Hello," he says.

"Hi," I say back.

But I can't do it. Even touching his back is revolting.

"Would you excuse me a minute?" I say. I step out of the room and get my jacket and other things from a closet in the hallway. I don't even risk waiting for the elevator, but bolt down the five flights of stairs. Needless to say, I never go back.

What do you think, Minnow? Is it unbelievable that I would go to work at a massage parlor? Maybe it never happened. Maybe in some other version of 1985, Lois and I said good-bye on the sidewalk outside Cafe La Fortuna, and I never called the number she gave me. Maybe I never asked her for the number. Maybe she never even worked at a massage parlor on lower Broadway.

But true or false, three years later, we run into Lois on the Upper West Side, and I introduce the two of you.

"Nice to meet you," you say.

"What a polite young lady," she says. "How old are you, Minnow?"

You hold out all your fingers on one hand and answer, proudly, that you're five and a half.

Lois looks better than ever, if that's possible. She tells me she's at Fordham, getting a law degree.

"That's so great," I say, truly impressed. We speak for a few minutes. She doesn't say anything at all about the past and neither do I. We make a silent agreement that any shameful or embarrassing thing we remember, about ourselves or the other, never happened. I look into those green eyes of hers, and we briefly embrace.

"See ya, Minnow," she says, walking backward.

It's the last time we ever lay eyes on her. She disappears into the world along with so many of the friends and acquaintances of my waitressing days.

You reach for my hand and we continue walking in the opposite direction.

Thirty-nine

By 1988, we've relocated from West Seventy-first Street to a floor-through in an old row house on Sixth Avenue in the Village. The location puts us in the right school district for you to attend one of the better public schools in the city. The new apartment has a slanted floor and a funky kitchen; the rent is an astronomical thirteen hundred a month. But my parents are contributing a small sum toward it, and I've got a new job, too.

Today we're back on the Upper West Side on our way to have lunch with Maria. We walk faster as we get close to our old building. You're excited to show Maria the dress you're wearing especially for her. It's pink and has a skirt like a tutu.

"Mama, is Maria going to be surprised to see me?" Your brown curls lift and fall as you skip along.

"No, baby. 'Cause she knows we're coming. She's going to be excited, though."

We approach the familiar front door, and you reach up to ring her buzzer.

I'm still climbing the last stairs as you run ahead to throw your arms around Maria's waist. She pats your back. "Hello, Minnow. Come in, you two."

Taking your hand, she leads you into the kitchen, where something smells good. Your voice is high and clear as you answer her questions about your new teacher, your school, and your pink dress. From her living room window I can see our former garden below. The old fencing has come down in one corner, and there are leaves from last fall covering the grass and flower beds. I wonder if the current tenants will bother to keep it up.

"How is the new job going, Lisa?" Maria asks, carrying a bowl of her special meatballs from the kitchen. She hands me a spoon. "Minnow, sit down at the table," she says to you. You carry your own bowl, carefully.

"I'm starting to get the hang of it," I say, about the job. I've recently gotten my real estate license at the suggestion of my cousin Rachel. I'm hoping to make some real money doing it.

I'm still at Silver one day a week, too, but since you started school, it's been increasingly difficult to work those hours.

"And what about the music?" Maria asks. "Have you been playing your guitar?"

"I have," I tell her. The new apartment has a back terrace that faces the beautiful old brick of another low building. Whenever I can, I sit out on there with my guitar and write. I watch the clouds roll past and sing my songs to the blue sky.

"That's good," Maria says. "Never stop."

"I won't," I say. But the truth is, it's hard to find the time. Days get eaten up by other things, or I'm too tired and crash out in front of the TV instead. I still love it, maybe more than ever, but it's not my priority. Not this time.

On Maria's table, the ceramic salt and pepper shakers are shaped like Hawaiian girls. You like to play with them, and she moves them closer to you. "Minnow," she says, "how is your Spanish coming along? Have you been practicing?"

"I'm a little busy right now," you explain, "but I'm still very good at it."

We smile at one another over your head.

"How do you say 'I love you very much'?"

"*Te amo mucho,* Maria," you say sweetly.

"Very, very good." She laughs appreciatively.

Maria's table feels like one of the safest places on earth. I think of the night that things got out of control with Corbin, when I grabbed you and escaped up the stairs. Her door was our salvation. She never said a bad word about Corbin. She never told me I was making a mess of my life.

When we go, we promise to come back soon.

"Can I sleep at Maria's house one day?" you ask me as we walk to Broadway to catch the train.

"Sure you can, baby. I think Maria would love that."

Forty

Every morning, I walk you to your kindergarten class, down
Sixth Avenue and right on Eleventh Street. You hold my hand.
Mixed into your walk is a little skip. You love to talk, non-
stop, for the pleasure of it, like a chirping bird. You ask questions about the trees, the weather, people who pass by, clouds,
the future, tall buildings, and more. When I don't know the
answer to something, we go to the Jefferson Library after
school and look it up.

"Mama, is that the horizon?" you ask one day, pointing
west toward the river. How do you know these things?

Another day you ask about a boy who is a bully at school.
"Maybe people haven't been nice to Sebastian, so he doesn't
know how to be nice to other people," I say to you about that
boy.

"You mean Sebastian's mommy and daddy?" you ask.

"Maybe," I say. "Or other kids might have been mean to
him when he was little."

You're quiet for a few seconds as you think it over.

We've had many conversations about *your* daddy, the first
when you were only three. You bring him up frequently, in
ordinary ways. I've told you he's very busy and lives far away.
I've said that someday when you're much older, you'll be able
to see him. I don't know if this is the right thing to say, or if
it's true.

You used to ask Corbin if he could be your daddy, but
Corbin is gone now, back to Austin. You still talk to him on
the phone sometimes, and you have your uncle Alan, and your
grandpa. You seem to be at least as happy and well adjusted as
the rest of the kids.

Alan continues to come by on Sundays when he's in town. You watch for him, pressed up against a window that looks out onto Sixth Avenue from the second floor.

Alan greets you with hugs and kisses. Sometimes he brings his girlfriend. She's a different one each time. It's hard to keep a relationship going when he's on the road so much. They're blond or brown-haired, or his favorites, the redheads. They're all young and skinny and a little self-conscious. They follow him up the stairs and hang back. Say hello with lowered eyes and stand in the corner or by the bookshelves, pretending to look at the titles. You're the icebreaker, Minnow. You're always so nice to them. You hold their hands and point out your drawings, framed in clear plastic on the long wall behind the dining table. You introduce them to the cats. You take them to your room and show them the papier-mâché sculpture that sits on your dresser. "See, it's a unicorn with wings," you explain.

They tell you you have pretty hair, or that they like your shoes, or your nail polish. When they ask you what you want to be when you grow up, you say a veterinarian, a scientist, or a mathematician. "I love prime numbers," you volunteer.

That usually throws them. They look dumbfounded. The first time I heard you say it, I was right there with them. I thought it must be something your grandfather had taught you to say; you've inherited his gift for logic and numbers. When I asked you what you loved about prime numbers, you said: "They're fun."

I don't know what it means to love prime numbers. But who am I to tell you what to love?

Alan still likes to take charge in the kitchen. He tastes the sauce and looks through my spices to add bay leaves or nutmeg or cinnamon. I'm happy to let him, though after all these years of his suggestions, I can cook almost as well as he can.

"Hey, do you ever hear from Jules?" he asks one Sunday.

Dave is there, too, that night. He's the bass player from Charlotte's band and Alan's good friend. It's just after midnight and Talk Talk's "Spirit of Eden" is turned down low. We're sitting around the long table, finishing up the last bottle of wine. "Yeah," I say, feeling a little drunk. "I'm in touch with her pretty regularly."

Renee, the current girlfriend, is resting her head on Alan's shoulder. I keep noticing the way her hennaed hair curls at the edges, the last of a grown-out perm. Beyond her through the open pocket doors, I can see you sleeping in my bed on a pile of coats.

"What's she up to these days?" Alan asks.

"She's still doing that television series, the medical drama. She plays the wife of the lead doctor."

"Oh, that's right," Alan says. "*L.A. Emergency.* I knew that."

"Which one is she?" Dave asks.

"The beautiful blonde," I say proudly.

Dave is impressed. "The one who accidentally kills her kid and has a mental breakdown?"

"Yeah."

"Say hi next time you speak to her," Alan says. "Tell her she's great on that show."

"I will." I yawn.

Alan stands and stretches. "Okay, time to go."

We watch Renee walk slowly across the long room to get their coats. She removes hers from under your head, carefully.

After they've gone, I lock up, turn off the stereo and the lights.

I carry you into your room and put you to bed. You pretend to stay asleep because you love to be carried. I used to do the same thing when I was a kid.

Your small bedroom, intended to be a dressing room, has no windows. It's dark except for the green glow of the night-light. I pull the covers up to your chin and kiss your warm head. "Good night, Minnow."

Your voice is sleepy and sweet.

"I love you, Mama."

Forty-one

Jules has always had a way with animals. Now she's got an injured blue jay in her house. She says the patient has a broken wing. She describes the way the other jays squawk outside the windows and beat their wings against the screens. When she steps outside, they do flybys, grab pieces of her hair. She thinks they aim to free the one she's nursing back to health. But then she leaves the door open for all the blue jays, and one brave bird, the leader, she suspects, flies in to check on his friend. He steals a bit of food from the captive's cage. After that, it's as if they understand she means no harm.

Minnow, isn't she just like a heroine in a children's book? A beautiful princess with a squirrel on her shoulder and a bird lighting on her outstretched hand?

As she tells me about the blue jays, I picture the house she rents in Santa Monica. I've only seen it in photographs. It's a Spanish-style hacienda with a red clay roof and a center courtyard with lush green plantings, colorful floor tiles, and a fountain. Light shines through big windows onto English pine dressers, large abstract paintings, a velvet fainting couch, a marble bust, two crystal chandeliers, her bed covered in the finest Irish linen. Even the vegetables on the kitchen counter seem more still life than salad. She shares the splendor with her beloved companion, a sensitive, geriatric Yorkshire terrier named George.

"What does George make of all the bird activity?" I ask. We've already been on the phone for forty minutes by then. I switch ears as she asks George what he thinks.

"George thinks everything should be about George."

We talk on the phone late at night. It's three hours earlier there, and she likes to stay up late. I can call her at four in the morning, New York time, and she answers after one ring.

Always, our talk turns to men. Jules is dating a powerful man in the movie business. He's married, so the relationship is hush-hush. He collects art and admires her good eye. They visit galleries together where she chooses the paintings, and he buys them for himself. It seems unlikely that he'll leave his wife and kids for her, but she says that's fine. She takes a painting class, cuts fresh flowers from her garden. She runs down to Mexico for a long weekend. And of course she's working. Doing a television series means long days and weeks. She says it's fun but exhausting.

I tell her my news. I've recently started seeing someone, too, a photographer I met at a Chris Whitley show. I describe the way we rip each other's clothes off and do it on the floor.

"Where does this happen?" Jules asks. She's never approved of my boyfriends.

"He has an apartment on Second and Tenth Street. It's a total crash pad. There's usually a roommate asleep on the couch."

"Charming," she says. "Has he met Minnow?"

"No, and he never will," I say. "Don't worry. I'm not serious about him."

"I hope you're being careful," Jules says. Careful. Because in the original 1988 when was I ever careful? Condoms, diaphragms, sponges, jellies, but always there were months when I relied only on prayer, as in: *Please, God, let me get away with it this time and I promise next time I'll be more careful.*

"Of course I'm being careful," I say now.

I'm about to turn thirty. So is Jules, but she's still got another two months left of being twenty-nine. It seems a momentous birthday, an age that requires I should have my life together. I've been torturing myself about my nonexistent musical career. "I feel like a big failure," I tell Jules.

"What are you talking about?" she says. "How are you a failure? You're supporting Minnow, building a real estate career. You're a talented songwriter and a great friend."

It makes me feel slightly better.

"And you're a goddess and a savior of birds," I tell her sleepily. It's starting to get light outside when we say good-bye.

Forty-two

In the original 1988, I open my eyes in Los Angeles, a city I'm unfamiliar with. It's hard to imagine that ten years later I'll buy a house here and know this city well.

I'm in town to meet the people at my new record company. They've put me up in a hotel just off Sunset and every morning I order the same thing from room service: a croissant with butter and jam, a pot of black coffee, and a pitcher of half-and-half.

Then I get dressed and pull on my brand-new cowboy boots.

The record company sends a car for me because I can't drive. I have my license, but I'm afraid. I'm afraid of getting lost in this strange city, afraid of missing an exit, or driving too slowly and being hit from behind. I'm afraid of so many things.

But my bank account has more money in it than it ever has before, thanks to a publishing advance. A bidding war has taken place between five record companies. Every day another major jumped in, making crazy promises that even in my total innocence I knew were too good to be true.

I signed with Harry Garfield for three reasons. One: he was the first to ask. Two: he'd signed some of my idols. Three: he said that we were going to make a record like Jackson Brown's *Late for the Sky* or Joni Mitchell's *Blue*.

Yesterday Harry Garfield walked me around to the various departments, introduced me to everyone; they smiled and shook my hand. They said they loved my songs and couldn't wait to work with me. Then Harry and I went to lunch and talked about choosing a producer. He made suggestions for how I could spruce up my image.

"Lose the backpack," he told me. I carry a black leather backpack with me that has my notebooks in it and whatever else I may need. I told him I didn't understand why I had to lose it. He smiled and shook his head at me. "You're such an *artist*," he said.

Somewhere in this city I know Gabriel is waking up. I haven't spoken to him in three years, but being in the same city makes me think of him.

I have a boyfriend, Tom, waiting for me back in New York, but that relationship seems doomed. When Harry Garfield met Tom he said I could do better, but I don't think that's why I've gone cold on him. I've tried to love him but I can't do it.

The car is late, so I sit down on the bed with my guitar. My Martin travels with me everywhere I go. I feel as if it contains the songs I've yet to write, or at the very least is a conduit. The guitar's warm rosewood body feels alive. It comforts me and keeps me from feeling lonely.

Forty-three

My father is teaching you to play chess. The two of you face one another across the board. When you take his knight, he says: "Very good."

Too excited to sit still, you jump up and do a little dance.

"Concentrate, Minnow," he says.

"Dad, she's a child." I hear myself sound like a nag. I'm watching from the hallway, between the den and kitchen.

My parents have moved, after twenty-five years, to another split-level house, in another Long Island town. It's free of history and ghosts. I like the way it feels clean.

I never learned how to play chess. My father attempted to teach me when I was a kid, but I had no interest in it. It seemed too complicated. I remember he invited a little friend of mine to play instead, which made me jealous, but I pretended not to care.

He ignores me now, and you grow still. Your lovely hair falls in nutty-brown waves over your face and shoulders. You've picked out the plaid jumper you're wearing and also the red shoes, the ones we call your Dorothy slippers. You're completely focused on the board as my father considers his next move.

I pour myself a cup of coffee and join my mother at the kitchen table. The weekend papers are spread out across it, *Newsday* and the *New York Times*. I find the Arts & Leisure section in the pile. If it's a test of compatibility to be able to sit silently with someone and read, my mother and I fail this test, addressing one another when we are most absorbed in what we are reading. We listen to the other's thought or observation, halfheartedly, holding a finger on an interrupted sentence, waiting to return to it.

You come running in, Minnow, and climb onto my lap.

"I won, Mama," you say, grinning. "Grandpa showed me how." One of your front teeth is missing. You've wiggled it free in the dark, excited to get a dollar from the tooth fairy.

My father is right behind you. He joins us at the kitchen table. I predict he will last no longer than five minutes. It's Sunday, and the pregame beckons.

"What can I get everybody?" my mother asks. She stands at the refrigerator, the door ajar. She is scanning the packed shelves for our midmorning snack.

"Pancakes!" you say.

"You don't want pancakes," my father says. "You just had breakfast."

"With chocolate chips?" my mother asks.

"Yes!" You jump off my lap and hop around the kitchen enthusiastically. "Pancakes! Pancakes!"

"If Grandma wants to make them, you can have pancakes," I say. I catch my father's disdainful glance, but ignore it and return my attention to an article I'm reading. It's about a recent scientific discovery. Evidently, every time a memory is retrieved, it is altered in the process.

"Pancakes, it is," my mother says.

Forty-four

After I walk you to school, I go to my office, which is just around the corner on Tenth Street off Perry. The neighborhood feels like a real village in the mornings, the scent of fresh bread wafting out over the street. I make a quick stop at the bakery for a coffee.

The sign above the storefront office reads CLARK AND WINSTON, REAL ESTATE—SALES AND RENTALS. Its elegant font is what attracted me to this particular agency. The bell on the door rings as I push it open, and the two owners look up. "Good morning," they say, almost in unison.

Barry and Arnie sit at opposite ends of the room, with a number of desks in between them. Neither one is named Clark or Winston. The name was chosen for the respectability it suggests.

"Good morning!" I say. I'm still new and trying my best to bring the correct enthusiasm to the job.

I've been fortunate so far. I have what everyone tells me is beginner's luck. It's hard to make a living doing real estate rentals. Nevertheless, I've rented two my first month and have a new client coming in this morning. She needs to find a one-bedroom before leaving town at the end of the day.

Arnie calls me over to ask me what I plan to show her. We go through my list. He makes a couple of calls and finds another apartment that has just come on the market.

When my client arrives, I stand and shake her hand. She's a busy young lawyer relocating from Boston to New York City. I introduce her to Arnie, who is wearing a nice suit but still comes across as sleazy.

I'm polite, professional, and dressed the part, still I feel like an impostor as I lead her back to my desk and hand her our registration form to fill out.

The young lawyer rents the first apartment I show her, a beautiful one-bedroom with casement windows and perfect wood floors on Christopher Street. My fellow agents can't hide their envy. They think my good luck is using up the supply. Arnie gives me a pat on the back, which gives him an excuse to rest his hand on my ass.

To celebrate my luck I pick up some day-old roses at the Korean market, along with the half gallon of milk we need. At home, on the way to the kitchen, I notice my Martin in its stand, unplayed and patient as a good dog. Maybe I'll sit out back on the terrace and try to write something, I think. I put the milk away, cut the stems on the roses, and glance at the clock. I've got ten minutes before I need to be at school to pick you up.

Forty-five

In the original 1989, my first record is released.

We drive across country, Alan at the wheel, Marianne Mercurio in back, her cello beside her like a fourth person. We play in what feels like every small club in every town or city that has one.

After sound check, we walk around trying to see into second-floor windows, wondering what it would be like to live in that particular city or town. Maybe we'll put down roots in Austin, we say, or Santa Fe, or Portland.

We stop for meals at fast-food restaurants along the highway, and stay in Motel 6s and weird family motels, where the first thing you do when you get into your room is strip the dirty coverlet off the bed.

We play a game where one person improvises a noise and the next adds a sound and it keeps building, layers of shifting harmonies, lip smacks, whistles, mouth drums, and humming, until something strikes us so funny, it ends in gasping, hysterical giggles.

The shows are the best part. It feels good to play, and momentum is building. Mitch, the head of marketing at Warners, calls. I can hear the excitement in his voice. The single is getting adds. "I wanted to be the one to tell you," he says, then lists the more than a dozen radio stations that are playing my record.

Every night there are a few more people in the audience than there were the day before. Suddenly we're playing for sold-out crowds. It seems to happen overnight. It energizes us through our exhaustion.

I wonder what Gabriel would think if he were standing in the crowd. When he hears my song on the radio—a song about him—does it make him miss me, just a little?

Sometimes I choose a fan-boy, the cutest one, and kiss him under a streetlight, or ride on the back of his motorcycle, or take him back to the motel. Always a part of me is thinking: *See Gabriel? Other men want me.*

Forty-six

Though most of what I know of him lives in my imagination, or in the past, or in your resemblance to him, Minnow, when

I fantasize in the dark, it's still Gabriel who plays the lover. Other boyfriends come and go, but Gabriel is like a hole in a tooth. My tongue likes to run over and over it. It's been years since we've actually spoken, but my memories of him play like a TV show in syndication.

I'm aware that his real life continues. Watching the Grammys a couple of years ago, I heard his name announced. He'd won in some obscure category, during the pretaping part of the show. And once, while waiting for you at the dentist's office, I read in a magazine that he'd gotten a divorce.

I know that the real Gabriel Luna still exists, but to me he's no longer an actual person. My fantasies have become more real to me than the man I knew.

So I'm stunned one day to see his name on a marquee at a supper club in Midtown. I believe the year is 1992. When I see it, I think, Could it be that easy? Simply buy a ticket and take a seat? The potential power of the experience frightens me. But I talk Alan into going and spend nearly two weeks' worth of grocery money on the expensive tickets. I feel like a dirty drug addict using that money. It's like I'm being controlled by a madness I thought I'd outgrown. I try to justify it. I tell myself that I need to see him to scold him for never taking an interest in you.

On the night of the concert, I leave you uptown with Maria. You sense my agitation and linger at the door as we say good-bye.

"Go have fun," I tell you. "I'll be back to get you first thing in the morning."

When I get to the club, Alan is already waiting for me out front. He is his usual happy, laid-back self and doesn't notice how charged up I am. We're seated at a small table right up front. I order a glass of red wine and finish it before Alan's

even taken a sip of his beer. I order another and drink half of
it down.

"Whoa, Nelly," Alan says.

I feel the warm confidence of the alcohol spread through my
brain and body.

While we wait, I look around. This is a completely different scene from the downtown clubs I used to frequent, before
you were born, where we paid five bucks at the door to stand
in a packed crowd, watching a skinny boy play guitar on a
makeshift stage. This place looks like it could be in Miami
or Cleveland or some place other than New York City. Everything is red and black. There are round booths against the
wall. People are dressed up, drinking and smoking, throwing
their heads back, laughing.

Downtown, there would be an opening band, or two, or
three. The headliner wouldn't come on before midnight. Here
there is no opener. Gabriel is scheduled to go on at eight, and
at eight-fifteen his band begins to play the intro to a song I
know from the first note. Instantly, I'm transported back to
1982, to the Vantage and the salsa clubs on upper Broadway.

A trumpet player I don't recognize steps up to his microphone and says, "Ladies and gentlemen, please put your hands
together . . ."

Gabriel walks out onto the stage and into the warm spotlight as his name is announced, nodding and smiling at the
applauding crowd. He holds a pair of maracas in one hand.
He's wearing the black-brimmed hat, a black T-shirt, and suit
trousers. He closes his eyes and lifts his face to the spotlight
as if in prayer. He moves simply and elegantly, a salsa step.
Front and back, and front, back, front.

He is almost the same. Almost. Although I think he's been
drinking. He seems less in control of himself. He avoids the

high notes. Between songs, he talks too long, more lecture than stage patter. A guy in the back starts to heckle him. "Enough talk, already. Shut up and sing!"

Surely, Gabriel can hear the comments, but if he does, he gives no sign.

"Shut up, yourself!" someone shouts at the heckler, and the guy grumbles but quiets down. I signal the waiter for another glass of wine.

Gabriel brings his talk to a rambling end and introduces a love song. As he begins to sing it, the room erupts in applause, and then gets pin-drop quiet.

I remember the song from when it was brand-new, sung in a seaside town called Githion. I close my eyes and see a rumpled bedspread, doors open to a terrace, our clothes billowing on a line like sails. Gabriel, brown from the sun, playing his small guitar with its stiff nylon strings. Someone had told us Githion was the true location for the story of Helen of Troy. I loved him like lungs love breath.

While he sings the love song, he looks out into the audience and his eyes seem to rest on mine. I'm almost certain he is blinded by the stage lights and can only see me in silhouette. Still, it makes my heart leap. I think, in that moment, if he asked me to, I would run away with him. I would pick up right where we left off.

But the thought leads me back to you. I reach into my bag and take your fourth-grade class picture from my wallet.

After the show is over, Alan and I linger at our table while the room empties. "I want to say hello to him," I tell Alan.

"Sure, let's go back," he says casually, unaware of quite how much it means to me.

I scribble a note on the back of a cocktail napkin and hand it to a guy who stands by the stage door.

Within minutes, Gabriel appears. "Hey!" he says. "Thanks so much for coming." He hugs me and shakes Alan's hand. Close up, he looks pale and tired. I catch my own reflection in the glass behind him and think I don't look much better. I'm flushed and puffy. My eyes are bloodshot from the wine.

"Great show, man," Alan says.

"It was amazing to hear the songs again," I say, thinking: Devastating is more like it. It's unreal to be in his presence after all this time, but I try to be cool.

We follow him backstage. "Amanda!" he says excitedly to a tall blonde leaning against a table. "This is Lisa Nelson, the best female songwriter I ever met!"

"Oh, hi!" She's got a southern accent, an American girl from Georgia, or someplace near. "I've heard so much about you," she drawls.

I shake her hand and introduce her to Alan. Gabriel holds on to my arm as he speaks briefly to all the others who have come backstage to see him. He introduces me to everyone as a great songwriter. They look at me with respect and it feels good, but what I want, more than anything, is for them all to go away so I can have him for a few minutes to myself. In my hand, I clutch your fourth-grade picture. You look so like yourself in it, confident smile and bright eyes.

Your father doesn't give me a chance, though. Time goes by and the alcohol is wearing off. I see him fading before my eyes. He starts to get his things together to go and asks Amanda for a pen. He hands me a scrap of paper with his number. "Call me tomorrow," he says. Amanda doesn't look worried. I guess she's not the jealous type, or maybe she feels certain that I'm no threat.

Alan and I leave through a back door under the red exit sign. The sidewalk is packed with theatergoers, and it's begun

to snow. I think about how excited you would be to see it falling and decide to ride uptown with Alan and surprise you at
Maria's.

On the subway, Alan mentions that Charlotte Winter is
looking for someone to open for her on a few dates, someone
who can travel light. "You could do it solo. Just you and your
guitar," he says.

It seems impossible to me, beyond my wildest dreams.
"Charlotte would never go for it. And even if she did, what
would I do with Minnow?"

"You could get your mother to stay with her. It's just a
couple of weeks. I'm pretty sure they're all East Coast dates."

"I don't know," I say, but the idea of it seems to shift from
completely impossible to merely unlikely. I think about the
songs I might play if, by some miracle, it were to actually
happen.

Forty-seven

At Seventy-second Street, we say a quick good-bye. Alan rides
on to the Ninety-sixth Street stop. I come up from the train
onto Broadway, amidst thousands of snowflakes floating down.
The wind is catching them up and swirling them around the
streetlights. As strangers pass, we smile at one another, sharing the beauty of it.

At Maria's door, you greet me in your pajamas.

"Get dressed! It's snowing," I say.

"Mom, we're watching TV." You're not as excited as I want
you to be.

"Oh, come on!" I say. "How often do we get to play in the snow?"

So you get dressed. Maria helps you on with your coat. "Don't stay out too long," she says.

Outside, we lift our faces to the falling snow. We gather it in handfuls. Everything is being covered in a pristine white blanket. You stick out your tongue to catch the fat flakes.

"Isn't it spectacular?" I ask you.

"It's freezing!" You have snow on your eyelashes. I think of that song from *The Sound of Music* about snowflakes on noses and whiskers on kittens.

You laugh up at me mischievously. You're making a snowball and want to hit me with it, but you don't want it to hurt. You toss it at my feet, giggling.

"Thanks for coming out to play with me," I say.

"You're welcome, Mom." What a lovely girl you are, Minnow. I want to remember this sight of you forever: ten years old, happy grin, snow in your hair. But you're shivering in your lightweight coat, and the wind is whistling in my ears. It's becoming a blizzard.

"Ready?" I ask.

"Yes!" you say.

"Let's get inside!"

Maria is waiting for us with hot, sweet tea. We huddle together on the couch and watch the end of a made-for-TV movie. I hold your ice-cube feet in my hands. Hector drifts in and out. We all agree the movie is stupid. Still, it makes Maria cry at the end, which makes us laugh.

After the movie, the eleven o'clock news comes on. They're predicting over a foot of snow will fall, and all the public schools will be closed. You dance around happily as Maria and

I make up the sofa bed. "Okay, time to calm down," I tell you. "Go brush your teeth. It's late."

"Listen to your mother," Maria says.

Forty-eight

In the morning the light hurts my eyes and I have a headache. I'm hungover from the three glasses of wine. I search through Maria's medicine chest for an aspirin, pop three Advil, and remember that Gabriel's number waits in my pocket.

I wake you and we get dressed. Maria asks us to stay for breakfast, but we're ready to go. We say our good-byes to her and race down the stairs.

Outside, the snow is deep and undisturbed. It takes a while to get to the subway. "Carry me!" you plead.

"You're too heavy," I say. "You can make it! Take big steps."

We shiver on the cold platform waiting for the express train to Fourteenth Street. By the time we get home, our feet are soaking wet and we're frozen. "Get right into the hot shower," I tell you. But you don't want to. You take off your wet boots and socks and climb into my bed. The cats meow and complain. I fill their water bowl and give them breakfast; put on a pot of coffee for myself. "Cereal or eggs?" I call to you.

"Pancakes," you say.

"Cereal or eggs?" I repeat.

"Cereal!"

As we eat our breakfast, I'm thinking about Gabriel when you say, "Does my father still live in Los Angeles?"

"Yes," I say, startled by our apparent telepathy. "Why do you ask?" It's been a while since you've brought him up.

"How old is my father now? What if he gets old and dies before I get to meet him?"

"He's not that old," I tell you, but I realize it's not something you're ever going to stop thinking about.

"My father's name is Gabriel and he's a singer," you say.

"That's right."

"Can we go to Los Angeles? I want to see him."

"You met him once," I say.

"I know. He bought me ice cream when I was a baby. But I don't remember him."

You look at me with a face that so resembles his.

"Let's see what happens, honey," I tell you.

Forty-nine

I run all the way from Fourth Avenue.

All morning, I've been working with a Wall Street trader who didn't like any of the luxury apartments I had to show him. He took his time wandering through the last place, pointing out its flaws. I kept checking my watch. Finally, he asked, in an irritated tone, "Am I keeping you from something?"

"Actually, I am late for another appointment," I said, kissing the commission good-bye.

Out of breath, I arrive ten minutes late at the French bistro on the corner of Eleventh Street and find Gabriel waiting out front in the cold. I remember one of his pet peeves is being kept waiting. "I'm so sorry I'm late," I say. "Why didn't you go in?"

He shrugs and grunts, but holds the door open, and I go through it.

We're seated in the back at a cozy table. The bistro is new and they've done a good job of it. It's comfortable and stylish with small marble tables; a large antique mirror hangs over a substantial oak bar. Gabriel doesn't notice or care. Our favorite restaurant, during the years we were together, was a neighborhood Cuban-Chinese joint where I learned to order dishes like *bistec salteado,* pepper steak, and *maduros,* sweet plantains. Its casual greasy food was the kind he liked best.

"So, what's up?" Gabriel wants to know. This is after we've ordered. I've told him about the real estate job, and he's described a house he's renovating in Malibu. We hold our coffee cups with both hands to warm them.

"Minnow wants to meet you," I say.

"Is she even mine?" he asks, quick and sharp. Dear Minnow, don't hold it against him. Human beings are so imperfect. You have his broad cheeks and intelligent eyes.

"You know she's yours," I say softly. We sit in silence for a couple of minutes. "She's a fantastic girl. She loves to read. She's incredibly smart. And she can sing."

He looks old and tired. How old is he now? Forty-six or forty-seven? Looking at him, I have this thought: During the time I first knew him, he was the best he will ever be.

Somehow, I convince him to come for an early dinner before he leaves for the airport the next day. I promise him he can leave after an hour if he wants to.

"I'll have to," he says. "My flight leaves at nine."

"Okay," I say. I remember when he used to miss his flights on purpose. He'd take too long saying good-bye, and then rush off, only to return an hour later to spend another night in my arms. *Ya te extraño,* he'd say. Already I miss you.

Walking back to the apartment, I think about how excited you'll be. I'm dying to tell you, but promise myself to wait. I don't want you to have too much time to worry about it. Still, when I pick you up that afternoon, the secret is showing on my face.

"What is it, Mom?" you ask. I try to pretend it's nothing but you won't stop asking. I make up answers to throw you off, but you can tell they aren't the real secret I'm keeping.

Finally, you wear me down. We've ordered a pizza for dinner. We're sitting at the table, the TV's going in the background, and I say it: "I met with your father today."

You couldn't look more shocked if I told you I'd had a heart transplant.

"He's coming here to have dinner with us tomorrow."

I see your wheels turning. "But I thought he lived in Los Angeles."

"He lives in Los Angeles, but he happens to be in New York right now. He has to go home tomorrow night, in fact. After he has dinner with us, he's going straight to the airport."

You don't say anything.

"What do you think?" I ask.

"What if he doesn't like me?"

My girl, it kills me to see my awful insecurity passed along to you. "Minnow, listen to me. He's going to love you. What's more important is that you get to decide if you like him."

You don't look convinced.

"Come here," I say, holding out my arms, but you're ten going on sixteen and don't want to be comforted by your mother. "I promise you, it's going to be great," I say, and reach across to tuck a stray nutty-brown curl behind your ear. "He's going to love you, and everything is going to be fine."

We spend the next twenty-four hours in a flurry of anticipation. We can't sleep. We aren't hungry. We don't want to go to work or to school. When we do go, we can't concentrate. I clean the house and shop for a special meal. You change your outfit three times.

"Stop," I say finally. "Why don't you read your book or watch a little TV."

"I'm too excited to read," you say, hopping on one foot.

Through the big windows that face Sixth Avenue, we see the snow start to fall. I can't remember another winter when we've had so much of it.

With your nose to the glass, you wait for him. "Mama, do you think he might not come because of the snow?"

"He'll be here," I say, and pray he will.

Right on time, the door buzzer sounds. You gasp and cover your mouth with your hands. *Calmate, mi amor,* I say, trying to calm myself, too. The Spanish words feel good on my tongue.

And there he is, standing in our living room: five foot nine or ten, hat in his hands, scarce hair standing on end, shining brown eyes that peek past heavy lids, broad, ruddy cheeks, a mischievous smile that exposes small, even teeth. "So, we meet again," he says to you, very dramatically.

"You don't know me," you say in wonder.

"Of course I do," he teases. "Don't you remember me?"

Instantly, you fall under his spell. "You bought me ice cream once, when I was a baby."

"That's true," he says. "You had a pointy head."

"No, I didn't!"

"Yes, I'm afraid you did. It was very pointy. It was so pointy, you could only wear pointy hats."

"Mom!" you exclaim, and look to me for verification that you never had a pointy head. I'm so moved by this silly ex-

change, tears are stinging my eyes and throat. I quickly wipe
them away with the back of my hand, shrug, and smile at you.

"I'm staying out of this," I say. I take Gabriel's coat. "Can
I get you a glass of wine?"

"Sure," he says, and then turns back to you. "Do you have
a boyfriend?" His teasing is warm and flirtatious. He's always
had a weakness for a pretty girl.

"No, I don't," you say. "I'm ten!"

"I'll bet you have two!"

It goes on and on like this. I light the candles and we sit
down to dinner: roasted chicken and mashed potatoes, glazed
carrots, and homemade corn bread. I watch the two of you fall
in love and your happiness fills me to the brim.

The snow is our accomplice. He calls to see if his flight is on
schedule, and it's been delayed. They say to check back in an
hour, so he stays for dessert. I pile scoops of vanilla ice cream
onto generous slices of warm apple pie.

Outside, the snow falls and falls, closing the airports and
sealing our fate. For tonight, at least, he is ours.

After dinner, he picks up my Martin, gathering dust in its
stand; sits down on my bed and tunes it quickly. You curl your
legs under as you take a seat beside him.

The song he sings is called "Baby's in Black." It's one of
his favorites, I remember, a song by the Beatles. His rhythmic
playing gives it a Latin feel. He shows you a harmony for the
chorus. "Can you remember that?"

"Uh-huh," you say, with serious eyes.

Your voices together blend into one, both reedy and strong.
The sound of it rings to the ceiling, beautiful and full. I ap-
plaud and whistle. After, you grin and look to him for what's
next.

"You wanna play something, Lisa?" Gabriel holds out the

guitar to me, and I take it from him. In my arms it feels like
a beloved pet left too long at the kennel.

Instead of playing one of my own revealing songs, I try to
remember another by the Beatles, one I used to play at the
piano when I was a kid. As I sing the words to "I Will," I
hear myself making a promise to wait a lonely lifetime, and it
feels painfully personal as if I mean every word of it. Gabriel
doesn't seem to notice. "Beautiful," he says, taking the guitar
back from me. "I love that song."

You stay awake for as long as you can, but finally, just before
midnight, agree to get ready for bed. "Gabriel, will you read
me a chapter in my book?" you ask him.

"Just one," I say. "It's very late."

You take his hand, and the two of you go together into your
room. I blow out the candles. The hot wax has burned down
the sides of the heavy candlesticks and pooled on the rustic
wood of the pine table. I clear the dessert plates and load the
dishwasher, wipe down the counters in the kitchen. When I
turn the water off, I can just make out his voice saying good
night to you.

Gabriel comes in behind me and places a hand on my shoulder. I turn to face him. We're standing so close I can smell the
wine on his breath.

"I better go," he says. We both know he'll never get a cab in
this blizzard.

"Thank you so much for coming."

"She's everything you said and more," he says. "I want to
help her. What does she need? Who pays for her school?"

"She goes to public school."

"I want to help her," he says again.

"Okay," I say, but I don't ask how or when. I dry my hands
and get his coat; walk him down the single flight of stairs to

the front door of my building. The plows are already coming up Sixth Avenue.

"Thanks for dinner," Gabriel says, adjusting his hat. "Where did you learn to cook like that?"

"Here and there." I can't help smiling at him, the way I always have. Even now, after everything, no one else makes me feel the way he does. When he kisses me good-bye, I lean into it. He still wears the same cologne and smells good. "Do you remember when you used to call me Pajarito?" I ask.

"Of course I do," he says. "You're still a little bird, just a little fatter one." His accent makes this sound more charming than you'd think. "I'll be in touch," he says, heading off into the snow.

I don't know why I believe him, but I do. After he goes, I climb the stairs back to the apartment, turn off the lights, and polish off the rest of the wine in the dark. I've spent way too much on it and the meal. I don't know how I'm going to stretch what's left in the bank for another two weeks.

Outside, the snow makes it feel as if the whole city is asleep, or maybe it's Gabriel's absence that makes the night seem so quiet.

Fifty

"Okay, here's the deal. You can open for us. There's just one small catch."

"What's that?" Alan has pleaded my case to Charlotte. Everyone in her band is a friend of mine. Still, I don't get the feeling she's a fan.

"She wants to take someone who can help with the equipment."

"What does that mean exactly?" I feel a little sick to my stomach.

"It means you might have to help with load-in, or whatever. It's just us and a tour manager, so everybody has to pitch in. But you know, it'll be fine. She's just being a dick."

"What do you think I should do?" I ask. It becomes more real as we talk about it, terrifying and exciting.

"You should do it," he says. "Don't worry about Charlotte. You need to get out and play." Alan has been bugging me to "get out and play" for a long time.

"I don't know," I say with a big sigh.

"Just say yes," Alan says.

So I agree to open for Charlotte Winter. Six dates over ten days. The calluses on my fingertips are practically gone, and I can't remember how to play most of my songs, but I think I can get it together, provided I practice every day. I have just two weeks to prepare.

They're not too thrilled about it at the office, but I've got one foot out the door of that place anyway. When I come back, I think I might go to one of the bigger real estate agencies, get into sales. But I don't want to even think about real estate now. Part of me hopes that once I'm out there, playing music, I'll never have to do anything else again. I know, realistically, there's no way we could live on the seventy-five dollars per show I'll be making. But I don't want to worry about that, or anything beyond this chance I have to play my songs for an audience.

After you go to sleep at nine, I work at the long table. Play and sing quietly. I make notes about capo placement, keys, and chord changes. I practice for hours, playing the songs in a changing order, trying to come up with a dynamic set. I want the first song to feel like the beginning of a story, and the last, a postscript. My fingers get sore and then become limber. My voice begins to open up. I polish the Martin and put new strings on it. I almost feel ready when the two weeks have passed, and it's time to go.

On the morning I'm to leave, we sit together, our bags at our feet, and wait for my parents, who are coming to pick you up. You'll spend two weekends at their house. My mother will bring you back to the apartment for the five school days in between.

The cats watch us warily. They know the suitcases are not a good sign. I've arranged for a friend to come by to feed them.

"I love our house," you say.

"I'm glad," I say. "I love it, too."

It really is a lovely place with its big windows and terrace, all your colorful drawings and the well-used furnishings of our life together in this open front-to-back room. It's my favorite of all the apartments.

"And I love Tiger and Kiki." The cats raise their ears when you say their names.

"I know you do." I think we're both nervous to leave, to be apart from one another and have our routine disrupted. We jump when the doorbell rings. "There they are," I say. For a second, I feel exactly as I used to when you were a baby and I had to go to work at the restaurant, when it was an agony to leave you. "Ready?" I ask.

"Yes," you say. You've got your heavy backpack over your shoulder.

My father comes through the door, all business. He rubs his gloved hands together and takes your bag. "Grandma's waiting in the car," he says. "Ready to go?" I hear his New York accent. He was born in the Bronx and raised in Queens.

I give you a big hug, breathing in the sweetness of you. "I'll call you later," I say. "Thank you, Dad." I put my arms around him, too. Then you're gone, and it's just me, alone with my terrible fear of performing and of being away from home.

I lift my bag to my shoulder and grab my guitar. Lock up the apartment and head toward the subway. I'm to meet Charlotte, Alan, and the others at the van rental place in the West Thirties.

They're already loading up the van when I arrive. Charlotte doesn't even say hello, just looks at the size of the bag I'm lugging and shakes her head. "I don't know where that's going to fit," she says, and gets into the passenger side of the van, in the front seat.

I exchange greetings with Alan, Dave, and JC, the drummer. They're friendly and warm enough to make up for Charlotte's rude welcome. The tour manager, a skinny road rat named Neal, comes around the side of the van, smiling, to shake my hand. "Is that it?" he asks of my big bag.

"And my guitar." My Martin is in its hard blue case.

"Okay, no problem." He takes the bag from me. The guys are unloading the van to reload it. Packing it up is a science. Guitars, amps, and drums fit together like puzzle pieces. They haven't done a van tour in a while. It's a downgrade from the bus they had last time. But they're cool about it.

Once it's done, we get in and go. Up the West Side Highway, New Jersey across the river, the George Washington Bridge ahead. Except for Charlotte, who doesn't say a word, spirits are high. Everybody laughs and talks. I sit in the farthest back and study our itinerary: Northampton, Boston, New York, Philly, Baltimore, and D.C.

Fifty-one

This is what it's like. They sound-check first. Charlotte, bitch that she is, drags it out for as long as possible, so I don't really have time to do a proper check. I'm not sure if she does it on purpose, but whatever her motive, I only get a quick line check fifteen minutes before I'm set to go on.

Every night I have to prove myself to the club owner, the soundman, and Charlotte's crowd. It's like they assume I'll be terrible. They make me earn every bit of respect. During the first couple of songs, I struggle. I can't find enough breath. My hands shake so badly I can barely hold them on the strings of my guitar. But at some point, around song three, the magic takes over. My voice sails into the crowd, carrying the pretty melodies and thoughtful lyrics of my songs, and I can feel the whole energy of the room change.

Someone yells: "Who are you?"

I say my name into the microphone and my ego makes a confused but happy recovery. The high of turning it around and connecting with an audience is pretty amazing. But I don't know, Minnow. I'm not sure I have what it takes to win over the world this way, one small club at a time.

After my forty-minute set, I go out into the audience and watch Charlotte and the band play. I get to know all of her songs and find my favorites. When she performs, it's like she's been taken over by an angel. Every night I almost forgive her coldness toward me. She's a good songwriter, and her voice is powerful. She can really play, too. She and Alan trade off licks. It's fun to see him doing what he was born to do. He moves his head and twists his mouth. Dave stands beside him, cool and solid on the bass. Nothing moves on him but his hands. And JC? Well, there's nothing sexier than a good drummer. I can feel his solid playing in my belly.

After they finish, we find a local bar and drink and talk until last call. Charlotte doesn't come with us. She's always worrying about her voice and goes straight from the gig to the motel. Neal says we were supposed to have shared a room, but she changed her mind. So I have my own, which is fine with me. The boys are all doubled up.

After the show in Boston, JC comes back with me to my room. But I'm so drunk, I can barely remember a thing about it, just the awkwardness of finding him asleep beside me when the sun comes up. Sober, we pretend that nothing happened.

Mornings, we fuel up on gasoline and coffee and hit the road. The drives are long. We live on fast food at the rest stops, pizza or burgers and fries, donuts and tacos. It leaves us feeling sick to our stomachs and still hungry at the same time. We're hungover, too. Or I am, at least. My skin hurts. I sip on a Coke to ease the nausea. After lunch, I close my eyes and try to take a nap as we drive and drive.

Coming into Philly, we hear the intro to Charlotte's single on the radio. We all sit up, get quiet, and listen. She sounds great, and the song is catchy and clever, but nobody else is playing it, evidently, and it turns out her record company has already dropped her. We find *that* out at our gig in New York City when nobody from her label shows up, and it explains a lot.

Including the new one, Charlotte's made three records for her label. She tells us the second didn't sell as well as the first, so the marketing department assumed this one would do nothing. They've spent hardly anything on advertising or radio promotion this time around. They're cutting their losses.

I remember being in the studio, in the original 1992. We were mixing my second record when I heard the news that Charlotte had been dropped. I'm sorry to say that my first reaction was: Better her than me.

"You only get so many chances," Charlotte says. "It's just the way it is." She seems to know it and accept it. But I think it's a shame; the new record is really good. It could be the one.

The Philly DJ back-announces her song and we cheer when he says her name. He mentions our show at the Tin Angel and tells his listeners what time they should tune in to hear Charlotte live. The rest of us have the afternoon off while she goes to the radio station to talk about the new record. Alan says he's going to take me to get a Philly cheesesteak.

I look at Charlotte's profile, her straight nose and strong chin, lit up by sunshine coming through the windshield. I admire the way she's able to do what she has to do, despite the disappointment. I realize she's tough because she has to be. I decide never to be mad at her again, no matter how rude she is to me.

Fifty-two

"How are you, Minnow?" I call you every day.

"Mom," you say. "Grandma took me to Petland and we played with the puppies and there was a parrot there that could whistle and say, 'What's up doc?'"

"What else is going on? How are things at school?"

"Fine," you say, but you want to talk about what you want to talk about. "They had mice and lizards there, too. And snakes. Mom, Grandma says I can get a guinea pig if you say it's okay."

"A guinea pig? Is that like a hamster?" I can't quite picture it. "We'll talk about it when I get home."

"But, Mom, they are so cute."

"Maybe," I tell you, thinking *no way*.

"But, Mom," you beg. Sweet voice, I miss you so much. In my dreams, you need me and I'm not there; you're in danger and I can't get to you.

My mother gets on the phone.

"Everything okay?" I ask her.

"Everything's fine," she says. "How's it going there?"

In daylight, the Baltimore club looks pretty rough. The walls are painted black and it smells of stale beer. "It's going great," I say. I see Charlotte giving me the evil eye. I should be helping with load-in. "I have to go, Ma. Give her a hug and a kiss for me, will you?" In the background, I can hear you still pleading your case for the guinea pig.

"Take care of yourself," my mother says. "We'll see you soon."

"Speak to you tomorrow," I say every day.

Fifty-three

We never get to be great friends, but on the last night, Charlotte Winter tells me I've worn her down like a mangy stray she's come to love.

"Thanks a lot," I say. I can't help laughing. I'll take what I can get. After hearing her play every night, I have a bit of a crush on her.

The D.C. gig is actually in Arlington, Virginia, at a club called Iota. The owners are feeding us and treating us like family. It's an early show, so the plan is we'll start back to New York after we finish. At a long table in the kitchen, we feast on veggie burgers and beer.

"But you know, you drink too much," Charlotte says. "I say that as a friend."

I'm shocked at this. She's sipping mint tea. She doesn't drink at all.

I don't think I drink that much. I have one or two before going on to take the edge off. I have a beer, or a glass of wine, during my set. After, I have a few drinks with the guys to be social. I don't drink more than anyone else in the band. Maybe she says it because I'm stoned, I think. JC and I have smoked a joint, and I'm a little out of it.

"You get sloppy," she says.

I think about the couple of times when, maybe, while I was playing I felt a little too loose, a bit out of control.

Alan comes to my rescue. "You kicked ass," he says. "You've definitely made some fans on this tour."

"I agree," says Dave.

"You rocked it," JC says, sounding more stoned than me.

"I'm just saying she should go easy on the beer," Charlotte says. "I didn't say she wasn't good." She lifts her cup of tea in the air. "To you," she says, and takes a sip.

"Thanks, guys." But I don't touch my beer after that. I can feel her watching me.

The club is packed when I go on a little while later. It's only six-thirty. I can't believe how many people have come out to see us play in daylight. My voice feels strong, my hands and fingers do what they're supposed to. The sound is good and the crowd is into it. Everything just comes together. I think it's the best show of the tour.

During the last song of my set, the boys get onstage. It's a thrill to have them behind me. They take the song to a whole other level. My heart is lifting right out of my chest. I drop to my knees and let out a wail. Someone in the audience shouts, "Yeah!"

During Charlotte's set, I'm out in front, singing along with the rest of the crowd, when she calls me up to the stage for her encore. I find a harmony, a third above her melody, and our voices blend as perfectly as blue and yellow make green. The crowd is on its feet and the band is rockin'. Charlotte smiles at me and I feel so high, I think, Who needs alcohol when there is music?

After the show, Neal settles up and herds us all out to the van. We load up and hit the road. Driving back, we're quieter than usual. Neal forgets to turn on the radio. We're looking forward to getting home and sleeping in our own beds. All I can think about is how much I miss you and that soon I'll get to see your face. I can't wait to tell you that I've thought it over and don't know a single reason why we shouldn't add a guinea pig to our family.

Fifty-four

"Mom," you say. "Listen to this one." You're in a silly mood, feeling giddy. You tell me a joke, and when I don't get it, you try to explain why it's funny through hysterical giggles. You're holding Z in your arms, the first of the guinea pigs. Turns out guinea pigs are social animals, so shortly after we brought Z home, we got Cinnamon to keep her company. A year has passed since we adopted the two of them.

"I'm sorry. I still don't get it," I say about the joke, and you give me a look that seems to say: *That's because you're old.* But I don't mind. You've been having a hard time lately and I'm happy to see you laugh and smile.

We go to Ray's, the pizza place on the corner, and I tell you about the time I came here when I was pregnant and had just seen the first-ever picture of you. You interrupt me to say, "I *know,* Mom. You've told me this a million times already."

"No, I haven't, not a million," I say.

"Mom, it's boring." You've become a teenager at twelve.

When we get home I notice that Kiki is not doing well. You're already dealing with a lot by then. You've just started the eighth grade at a private school Gabriel insisted was the best. You miss your friends and are having a hard time adjusting.

All the way to the animal hospital, you beg the taxi driver to go faster. Kiki is weak and thin. She hasn't been eating, not even the tasty bits of tuna we held beneath her nose. An hour after we bring her in, she's gone. We stroke her side and say her name as the veterinarian administers an injection to end her life.

After, you sob, your arms wrapped around my neck. "*Why,* Mom?" you ask.

"She was very sick," I tell you gently. "But she had a good life and she's not suffering anymore." It's all I can do not to break down myself.

We hold hands on the way home. For a few hours, you become my baby again.

Fifty-five

Before we've even had a chance to mourn Kiki's passing, Hector calls with the news that Maria has suffered a stroke. Tragedies seem to come in bunches, Minnow. I don't know why it's true.

We go to visit Maria on the Upper East Side, at the hospital where you were born. She's already been there a week, and Hector says she's doing better.

You hand him the flowers we've brought and he thanks us for coming. "Where's Maria?" you ask.

"She's with a physical therapist," Hector says. "He's got her up and walking."

This sounds encouraging, so we're shocked to see her when she's brought back to the room and helped into bed.

Maria seems to be paralyzed on her left side. Her mouth drags down and her eye doesn't blink. Her arm hangs at her side. Hector lifts it at the elbow and arranges it in her lap. He adjusts her pillows to make her more comfortable.

Thankfully, though her voice is weak, she can still speak, and she says, "Minnow, it's so nice of you to come visit me. *Ven acá.* Sit. Hector, get a chair for Lisa."

Hector goes out into the hallway to find a chair for me. Maria directs you to her good side. You sit beside her, on the edge of the bed. *"Mi amor,"* she says, "you look wonderful. How is school?"

Her illness makes you shy at first, but soon you're telling her about your teacher and your friends, just the way you always have, leaning in close. She reaches up to touch your face with the palm of her good hand.

In the next bed, behind a curtain, another woman clears

her throat. She has no visitors. When a nurse comes in and pulls the curtain back, we see she is a tiny old woman, gray and frail. "Hello, there," I say to her brightly. "Can we get you anything?" She slowly shakes her head no.

"You're a good person, Lisa," Maria says to me softly, and it almost makes me cry because she is so kind and so sick.

We treat Maria's bedside like it's the living room in her house. We play cards and talk. Even the dust particles hover around her in the sunlight. We learn that she will be released soon; she'll go to a rehab center in order to regain the use of her left side. Her doctor says that if she works hard, there's no reason why she can't make a full recovery.

When Maria's son and grandsons come to visit, we've already been there for more than an hour. So we leave to make room for them. You tell Maria you hope she feels better soon. We kiss her cheek and say good-bye.

On the way home, you ask me to explain what has happened to her.

"Maria had a blood clot," I say. "It caused the part of her brain that controls her left side to be damaged, but the brain is an incredible organ, and it can learn new ways to do the things it used to do."

You're fascinated by this and want to learn more about the brain. We go to the library and check out books about neuroscience. I've got Oliver Sacks's *The Man Who Mistook His Wife for a Hat.* You choose a medical journal called *Clinical Neuropsychology: Brain and Behaviors.*

"Mom," you say as we're getting ready for bed that night. "I'm glad Maria's stroke was in the right hemisphere and not the left. She could have lost her ability to speak and understand language. That would have been terrible."

I lean in to kiss you, and you allow a brief brush of my lips on your cheek, the last of good-night kisses. You're separating from me. I understand it, because I've been doing research about that, too. Though it hurts to have you recoil from my touch and dismiss my opinions, I've learned that individuation is the process by which a person becomes her true self.

Fifty-six

"You know the face you see in the mirror when you first wake up," Jules says. "The face with its creases and droopy eyes? Well, one day it just stays that way. It's your new face!" We laugh hard over that one. Tears of mirth roll down. It seems exactly true, terrifying, inevitable, and hilarious. We're still young but don't know it.

Jules has called to tell me about her reunion. The cast and crew of *L.A. Emergency,* the show that kept her employed for six seasons, has had a party to mark another six since being canceled. She tells me how good it was to see everyone, talks about them all by first name—her fellow cast members, the writers, producers, assistant director, second assistant director, caterers, grips, makeup artists, and so on. "We were like a family," she says, and sighs.

I ask about her current work prospects. She says she's had a couple of good auditions, but hasn't heard back yet. "How are things at your job?" she asks.

"Unfortunately, I don't think it's going to be canceled," I say.

"Oh? I thought it was going well," she says.

"It's fine." How to explain the tedium of it to her? She's

under the impression that it might be fun, like a TV show about a real estate office. "It keeps Minnow in jeans and T-shirts," I say.

"Is Minnow still having her dinner dates with Gabriel?"

"Yes," I say, and lower my voice so you won't hear. You're in your room doing homework. "He's been taking her to all his old haunts when he's in town. I'm sure it's the Gabriel show, but she doesn't seem to mind."

"Oh, she must be mad for him," Jules says. "Getting to know him after all these years?"

"You never liked him much," I remind her.

"I didn't? No, I guess not. I never liked the way he treated you."

When she says this I suddenly remember a time that the three of us went to the movies together and, in the dark, I saw him put his hand on her knee.

Fifty-seven

At thirteen, Minnow, you excel intellectually. Socially, you're warm and outgoing but easily bruised. You come home crying after school because the girls have arranged themselves into cliques and excluded you. The mean girls know how to find your weakest point and prey upon it.

One day, they make fun of your favorite shoes, and you refuse to wear them. You say you have to have new shoes, just like all the other girls, so we go shopping for them on Eighth Street. "They have to be exactly the same, Mom. Not a bargain brand," you warn me. When we get home, you take the new shoes from their box to dirty them up. You step on them, bend them, and otherwise abuse them, trying to make it look as if you've had them for years. Then you put them on and look at them from all angles in the full-length mirror on the back of the bathroom door. "What do you think?" you ask me.

I could laugh or cry. "They look nice," I say, and you frown because my response is not the enthusiastic one you want.

Most of your schoolmates have parents who are wealthy and divorced. Chic mothers and absent fathers. In this, you are the same. Gabriel calls to speak to you on Fridays. His check comes at the beginning of the month. He wants to see report cards and hear progress reports. He doesn't take his investment lightly.

In the years since your first meeting, I've watched your relationship with him grow, though he continues to be himself, busy and self-centered. You bend toward him like a lily hoping for a little more sun.

When he calls to invite us to spend the month of August at his house in Malibu, how can I refuse? We go to see him in Los Angeles, just the way I've always told you we would.

While you have surfing lessons and get dragged along to business lunches in Hollywood, I make the drive to Santa Monica to see Jules.

It's hard to be an aging beauty, and harder still to be an aging beauty in Hollywood. Since her TV show was canceled, Jules is playing the occasional mommy now and is glad to have the work. She's no longer an A-lister and says she couldn't care less. She sees the entertainment business for its superficialities and says she doesn't take the rejection personally. She's happy for the time her frequent unemployment gives her to paint and work in the garden. But being without money is another story. She's not good at it. She's not the kind to stretch a penny or forgo a purchase. She's no longer living in the Spanish hacienda, but coming up with the rent, even for her more modest house, is a challenge. When I go to see her in Santa Monica, I've just left Gabriel's place, where the phone is still ringing with opportunity.

I pull up to her charming cottage surrounded by pink rosebushes and palm trees in Gabriel's silver Mercedes convertible. She comes running out, letting the screen door slam. "Hi! Fancy wheels!" she says. She's laughing, and her five Chihuahua rescues are on her heels, barking. The sun is shining through her gold hair. She seems illuminated. I jump out of the car and throw my arms around her. It's the first time we've been face-to-face in more than ten years.

Her house smells of laundry soap and coffee. One of the dogs isn't quite housebroken yet, and Jules's bedding is in a constant state of being washed or dried. There are piles of sheets and blankets on a tabletop waiting to be folded.

All of her beautiful furnishings and collected objects are crowded into the rooms of this smaller house, arranged in artful groupings, displayed as if in a gallery or shop. Still, there's no place to sit down, really. She leads me through the hallway, the living room, and dining room. The dogs follow, causing commotion and chaos. She scolds them affectionately.

In her yellow kitchen, the sun shines through a window above a white cast-iron sink. On the counter two large enamelware canisters catch my eye: SUGAR and FLOUR. Jules pours freshly made coffee into heavy mugs, and we sit at the table. We could be back on Tenth Street, at her old place in the Village. "What's going on with you and Gabriel?" she asks.

"Nothing," I say. "It's all for Minnow." Although it is nice to spend time with him again.

"How is our darling girl?" Jules asks, and I explain that

since Maria's stroke you've become fascinated with the brain and now want to be a neurologist. I describe the way you took to your surfboard with a fearlessness that astounds me. I tell her that, a few months ago, you got your first period.

"Oh, it starts," she says.

"The only concern I have, really, is the way she worships Gabriel. I hope he doesn't let her down."

She looks at me knowingly, and I know what she's thinking: Like mother, like daughter. But you're not like me, Minnow. You're able to love more than one thing at the same time.

I ask Jules about the movie-business mogul, the one she will later refer to as the love of her life. She says she still hears from him occasionally. "He couldn't deal with the dogs," she says as she gets up to let them out into the yard. "We grew apart." She lights up a cigarette, that most familiar of her gestures, cupping the match, although there is no breeze.

I wonder if there were other things about her he couldn't deal with. She is bigger and brighter than she was. Like a child's colorful drawing, she's made no effort to stay inside the lines. It occurs to me that this behavior may only be socially acceptable in the young. With age, it seems more like eccentricity or madness.

After we finish our coffee, she takes me out back to her studio, a converted garage with white walls, a large skylight, and a concrete floor. The room is full of her artwork and supplies. One large canvas has a vintage ball gown affixed to it. It stands six feet tall. Another is a self-portrait that captures her features but lacks her essence. Her real face is so animated, eyes squinting or opened wide, brow furrowed, mouth moving in explanation. "What do you think?" she asks, striking a match to another Marlboro Light.

"I love this," I say, approaching a piece in the corner. She's constructed what looks like a beehive in the shape of a woman's torso. Patches of chicken wire show through plaster or molded paper. It reminds me of your unicorn with wings, Minnow, the one we made when you were five.

"This one is a work in progress," she says of the six-foot dress.

"It's beautiful, as is," I say sincerely, but there's something sad about it. It reminds me of an abandoned bride. So I ask her, "Do you ever get lonely? Do you miss him?"

"I think about him," she says, "but I'm too busy to get lonely. All the time I used to waste thinking about him, I spend on my work now, and it's not just time. The *quality* of my entire focus is different. I don't have the distraction of wondering what he's thinking or doing, or when I'm going to see him next." The room fills with a cloud of her cigarette smoke, and I move toward the door for air.

The five little dogs bark and follow us back to the house. They burst through the kitchen door when she opens it. *They* must distract her, I think. Life is full of distractions. Still, nothing throws you off course like the obsessiveness of love.

But would life be worth living without it?

Fifty-eight

Gabriel and I drift together in August. After you've gone to bed, we stay up late talking. In the morning, watching you swim out too far, we reach for one another in worry. Our love for you is a magnet that draws us close. We sit out on the deck in the mornings and read the paper, the way we once did on the Upper West Side. He's still infuriated by all the political corruption and stupidity in the world. He's still threatening to do something about it one day.

We drift together, more out of proximity than love. He'd say I should speak for myself, that I never could appreciate how much he cared for me. He'd say he remembers everything differently. But what *I* remember is one night he pulls me into his room, half joking. "Tonight, you sleep in the big bed," he says.

Laughing, we fall into each other's arms. But, Minnow, it's strange. No matter how vivid the memory, or great the longing, when you try to go back, you discover you can't. We look for the way it was, the way we once fit, the way it used to feel. But it's as if the past is a ghost floating above the two of us. We're strangers now, saying strange things. His touch is different. It's been affected by other lovers, and I've lost the knowledge of his body, his likes and peculiarities. So we're two changed people in his big bed, awkwardly making love, pretending we remember how.

When I open my eyes the next morning, I wonder if my attachment to him has been reignited and escape into the bathroom wrapped in a sheet. At breakfast, I direct my attention to you and your plans for the day. I avoid his glances. But within a day or two, it's almost as if it only happened in a dream.

Nearly every afternoon, the house fills up with his friends, business associates, and hangers-on. He's always drawn people to him like flies to meat. They bring offerings of rum and tequila, six-packs of beer. He talks and drinks while they listen and laugh. He regales his friends from New York with funny stories about the old days and promises his Latin American compatriots that one day soon he is coming home, and when he does, "There are going to be some changes, man. I'm telling you. You watch." For emphasis, he snaps his thumb against the middle one. It makes a loud sound like a crack.

I can't tell if his friends believe him or only want him to think they do.

Sometimes Gabriel confuses me with the memory of his wife or other girlfriends. He repeats things that they've said and attributes them to me. He says, remember when such and such happened? And I don't remember, because I wasn't there, because it wasn't me.

None of his other women have given him a child, though. You come running toward us, brown from the sun, your long, wet hair full of sand and seaweed. You're so beautiful, it leaves even Gabriel speechless. No one else has ever given him anything that compares to you.

"Wipe your feet before you go inside," he says.

"Okay," you answer, stopping short. We watch you quickly brush the sand from your legs and feet with a towel. Your skin is the color of warm clay. You throw us a happy smile over a brown shoulder. You're having the summer of your young life.

Gabriel's house is modern and clean, ten times the size of our apartment. Your room, on the second floor, has a canopy bed and French doors that open to a terrace with a view of the Pacific Ocean. I watch you begin to take it for granted, just a little, and think: Good. I want you to be comfortable with beauty and privilege. You already know how to be poor and get by.

At sunset, we walk along the beach. The light is turning everything pink and gold. Up ahead, there are rocky cliffs with houses built upon them. From this distance, it looks as if the houses sit perilously close to the edge.

"Mom," you say. "They look like they're going to fall into the ocean."

"They do," I agree.

And one day they will, although I don't tell you that. One day everything we know will be gone, taken by mudslides, erosion, or time. But life is resilient. New houses will be built upon the ruins and other girls will walk this stretch of beach.

Too soon, it is the end of August. On another perfect sunny day, we pile into the Mercedes and Gabriel drives us to the airport. I'm excited to be going home, but fear once we get there we're going to miss your father's larger-than-life antics, his funny stories and meandering explanations. We sing along with the radio at the top of our lungs. When another driver tries to cut us off, Gabriel jokingly screams and curses at him in Spanish. "Cover your ears," I tell you, and you roll your eyes.

At LAX, we pull up to the curb at departures and Gabriel turns to you in the backseat. He hands you a twenty-dollar bill. "Minnow, you see that porter right there?"

"Uh-huh," you say.

"Well, you give him that twenty before he takes your bags. Then he's going to treat you right. You hear me?"

"Yes."

"Yes, what?"

"Yes, Papi." This is what you've agreed to call him, but it's hard for you to do it with a straight face, and it never takes.

We get out of the car, and he scoops you up in his arms. "You my girl?" He kisses you and squeezes you, too tightly.

"Gabriel!" You squirm and laugh. "Put me down!"

"See you soon, kid," he says, rubbing your hair. He walks toward me. "You got everything?"

"All set," I say, lifting our bags from the trunk of his car. "Thanks again."

"One day, it's going to be you and me," he says, placing his hand on my shoulder. "When we're sixty, after I finish every-thing I have to do. It's gonna happen, you'll see." He plants a wet kiss on my cheek. When he's sixty or when I'm sixty? I wonder. What a crazy thing to say. Then I remember he'll forget he's said it, even before he drives away.

Your father gives us a wave and jumps back into the Mer-cedes. He revs the engine, honks the horn, and he's gone.

Fifty-nine

In the original 1995, at the end of summer, I go to see a doctor on the Upper East Side. Dr. Marshall is my sister's gynecolo-gist, a specialist in the field of infertility. I've come to see him to find out why my period is so irregular. I haven't gotten it in more than three months. Dr. Marshall is an elegant gray-haired man with an Eastern European accent. He tells me to get dressed and meet him in his office.

Facing him across his desk, I tell him that, at first, I felt certain I was pregnant.

Dr. Marshall clears his throat. Gently, he tells me that he's certain I was not, because I'm done. I won't become accidently pregnant again. He looks directly into my eyes. "I get so angry at these men who take up the most important years of a wom-an's life," he says. "It makes me furious to think about their selfishness!"

What's the big deal? I think. Don't make such a fuss. I want to shut him up, to tell him that I'm not like most of his patients, desperate to become a mother.

Still, once I leave his office, I find the news has left me

numb. I stop for a bottle of red wine on the way home to have with dinner.

I was three weeks in Asia on a promotional tour, walking the streets of Tokyo, Hong Kong, and Singapore, thinking that I didn't have time to be pregnant. Although it was interesting to feel that I wasn't alone, my imaginary fetus with me as I visited temples and markets, played odd venues, and returned to my hotel. I wonder if could? I thought. How would I manage it?

On the day I was to leave for Asia, Arthur, my off-and-on-again boyfriend, producer, and drinking buddy, asked me to meet him on Madison Avenue in front of Cartier at nine in the morning. He was going to buy me a ring. It was a grand gesture. We'd get married, he said, but I didn't believe him; nor was I sure I even wanted to. I couldn't imagine Arthur as a father. Cartier didn't open until ten anyway. We waited for fifteen minutes in the rain, then abandoned the whole idea to go get breakfast.

I drink the bottle of wine and leave my dinner's ingredients to spoil on the kitchen counter. I watch TV, flipping through channels, looking for something of interest, something to push Dr. Marshall's diagnosis to the back of my mind. *There will be no more babies, not to have, or to flush down the drain.*

Sixty

In his old age Tiger spends his days asleep in a chair. Goldy, the fish won last summer in a street-fair game, seems to watch from her bowl. Z and Cinnamon, the guinea pigs, play and groom one another. It's a good thing the animals have each other for company. Because although you love them, they might wither from neglect waiting for you to come home. At fourteen, you have homework, after-school activities, and a busy social life.

My day begins early. I wake you, feed the animals, and make breakfast. The phone is ringing before nine. I've got a day of appointments ahead and usually need to go by the office first. The market in New York City is heating up in the fall of 1996. Anyone with an ounce of ambition would be selling co-ops and condos by now, but I'm stuck in rentals. I'm not a natural salesman and still have trouble pretending to be one.

On Tuesday nights, I host an open mic at a coffee shop on Tenth Street called Joe's. I look forward to it all week and always try to have a new song to play. There's an unspoken rule at Joe's that the songs should be fresh—written during the previous week.

The same core people come each week, along with others who arrive early to add their names to a sign-up sheet and wait their turn to play two songs. The cappuccino machine interrupts the mood so frequently that we no longer notice it.

Late in the evening, the regulars stick around to play longer sets. One boy, Jude Blake, has a talent so powerful that he begins to garner a buzz. Joe's is a tiny place, a storefront with a long counter and a few chairs. Jude fills it to the rafters. This kid plays his chest like a beat box. He sings like Nina Simone or Robert Plant. He's funny and as beautiful as a girl. A&R guys from all the record companies come to hear him play. Some keep coming even after Jude gets signed. They assume the room itself must be magic.

I'm thirty-eight that year, trying to pass for twenty-nine. My face is beginning to give me away. It's the first year I'm no longer pretty, in that pretty-girl way.

One night, I take Jude home with me and we're making out on the bed. You're at Jill Woo's, where you spend more and more time. She's your best friend, a tall, beautiful Chinese American girl.

Jude has his hand down my pants when he tells me he's in love with another singer. We continue to fool around for a minute, but then I push his hand away.

"What's wrong?" he wants to know.

"I think I'm just not in the mood for this," I tell him. After he goes home, it hits me. Young men won't necessarily fall in love with me anymore, at least not the shiny ones like Jude Blake. I'm thirty-eight and the rules have changed.

At Joe's, I play my songs after I've introduced a lot of other songwriters and they've played their songs. I try to treat each person well, to be generous and professional. I'm rewarded with respect and a small following of my own. People request favorite songs, and when I play them, the room goes silent. It's a beautiful thing to be listened to, to be heard. I play a song written for my sister, called "Another Year."

> Take the memories off the line,
> Put them in a pile of yours and mine.
> They've been bleached out by the sun,
> They don't belong to anyone . . .

When I sing it, I think of her, three years old, on Christmas morning, wearing an army helmet. She's living in Connecticut now. She's got two kids of her own.

I'm working on a new song that's about the way the past doesn't always feel like the past. I'm hoping to finish it in time for next week:

> Someone says the past no longer exists,
> But I don't think it's so . . .

One Tuesday night, I see Alan coming through the door and jump up to greet him. Some of the other songwriters get on his nerves, so he doesn't come to Joe's as often as I wish he would, but when he does, he brings his guitar. Having Alan play on my songs is like putting them in a beautiful frame. He makes me look good.

That night, an A&R guy from an independent label called Church Records happens to be in the room. In the 1990s independents aren't so independent. They're all financed by the big record companies and have access to real distribution, radio, and marketing. Plus, they have a cachet that the big labels lack.

Harry Garfield is about my age, a music fan. He dresses fashionably and has a good haircut. He's been in the business a long time already. He started his career at Warner Bros., and then went to Chrysalis, before landing at Church. He hasn't signed anyone of note lately, but he's still given a lot of leeway.

He approaches us at the end of the night. I'm breaking down the PA, something I do every week. The guys who work at the coffee shop carry the heavy speakers to the basement. Alan is watching me wind cables, telling me I'm doing it wrong.

Harry Garfield comes over, holds out his hand, and introduces himself.

"I think we've met, man," Alan says, "when I was playing with Charlotte Winter."

"Oh, yeah, yeah," Harry says. "What's Charlotte up to these days?"

I want to kick Alan. Doesn't he realize Harry Garfield isn't here to talk about Charlotte? She's without a record deal herself now.

"She's writing," Alan says. "Working on new material."

"Uh-huh," Harry says, but he's looking at me. I'm careful

not to stand in the unflattering overhead light. If I'm twenty-nine, there's still time to have a career. "You're so good. Why haven't I heard of you?" he asks, shifting from one foot to the other.

The confused excitement in my chest makes it hard to speak. I'm thinking so many things at once. *It's because I'm not really good enough. Because I've got a fourteen-year-old daughter I'm raising by myself. It's because I haven't ever really tried.*

But what I say is: "*I'm* here every week. Where have *you* been?" It comes across as jaunty and charming, and I can tell he's buying it. He thinks I'm cool and pretty. He likes my songs and the way I sing them.

He takes a business card from his wallet. "Call me," he says. "Let's figure out a time for you to come up to the office."

I let my hair fall over my eyes. I'm playing someone I think I should be, channeling Juliette Binoche, maybe, in *The Unbearable Lightness of Being*. "I'll do that," I say, and take the card from his hand. I put it in the back pocket of my jeans and pretend it doesn't matter to me that much, one way or the other.

Sixty-one

The apartment is dark when I get home. I turn the key in the lock and push the door open. I'm reaching for the light switch when I hear the sound of frantic rustling coming from my bed.

Oh, no, I think. Minnow, do you have a boy in here?

My panic is quickly replaced by surprise as I flip the lights on and see you and Jill scrambling into your clothes. "Mom," you say. "Do you *mind*?"

I'm so stunned; I don't know what to do. "Sorry," I mumble, and go into the kitchen to give you your privacy.

The secret lives of teenage girls. I think of the lined pages of my diary at fourteen, filled with the details of my own mother's worst nightmare. I put on a pot of water for tea, stand in the kitchen, and wait. I hear you saying good-bye to Jill, the sound of the front door opening and closing.

"Do you want a cup of tea?" I ask, facing the scratched sink and worn cabinets. I envision the conversation we will have, sitting at the table, mother and daughter. Unlike my own mother and me, we are open with one another. We can tell each other anything.

But you don't answer, and when I poke my head into the room, I find it empty. You've gone into your own room.

"Minnow?" I tap softly on your door.

"I'm sleeping, Mom," you say.

"Okay." I pause. What should I do? Must I wait for you to initiate the conversation? I hope you don't feel embarrassed or ashamed. "Good night, honey," I say.

"Good night," comes your sweet voice through the door.

I carry my tea to the table, turn on the TV with the volume low. There are always wars, and fires, and other catastrophes to provide distraction. Tiger jumps into my lap. I scratch his belly, and he purrs like a motorboat. On the news, a family has been rescued from a fire in Queens. They stand together in front of a house in ruins. A handsome firefighter denies he is a hero. I sip my hot tea, thankful for the roof over our heads, feeling the fatigue of the long day.

I wonder if I'd be so calm if I had caught you with a boy, instead? At least the encounter with Jill Woo can't leave you pregnant, and girls experiment, I think. It doesn't mean, necessarily, that you're gay. Of course, if you are, Minnow, I'm okay with it. You know that, don't you?

In the morning I wake you and you hop into the shower while I start breakfast and see to the menagerie. I'm hoping there will be a minute or two to talk, but then the phone starts to ring, and it's getting late. You grab your lunch from the refrigerator. "Bye, Mom."

"Will you be home after school?" You're already half out the door.

"Nope," you say. "I have basketball and then some of us are going to Jill's."

"Will Jill's mother be home?" I ask, and regret it instantly.

"Yes," you answer, running down the stairs. Is it my imagination or is the one syllable infused with shame?

It's not until the following Sunday, waiting for your grandparents to arrive for brunch, that the time seems right to broach the subject. By then, our conversation feels forced and awkward.

"Look, Minnow," I say to you. "This is getting ridiculous. We need to talk about it."

You're holding one of the guinea pigs in your arms, stroking her soft black-and-white fur. "There's nothing to talk about," you say.

"I think there is," I tell you gently. "I think you're feeling embarrassed about my walking in on you the other night."

You rub your face against Z's back and don't say anything.

"Am I right?"

"I don't know."

"Isn't there anything you'd like to say to me about it?"

"Sorry I was in your bed." Your brown eyes are wet with tears. You're trying to blink them away.

"It's okay," I say, as lightly as I can.

We sit quietly for a few minutes, and then it comes out.

"I like Jill, but she doesn't like me." The tears are rolling down your cheeks, and I want to hug you, but force myself to sit where I am and listen. You wipe them away, holding the palm of your hand against one eye, your long hair falling over your face.

"There's a boy from school she likes—Josh."

"She seems to like you very much, too," I say.

You don't respond to this, but sigh deeply. "Not the way I like her," you say finally.

The doorbell rings. "Go throw some cold water on your face," I tell you. The brief conversation has us both feeling a little better, and you give me a brave smile.

I buzz my parents in and watch from the doorway as they ascend the stairs.

"Hi!" my mother calls. "We lucked out and got a parking space right out front."

"Good for you," I say, holding the door open, kissing them.

"Where's my girl?" my mother asks, and you come out of the bathroom, smiling. You kiss them and hug them.

Your grandfather is not as affectionate with you as he was when you were small, but that's just how he is. Grown-up girls aren't as easy for him to make sense of. "Hi, Minnow," he says in his soft alto. His hair is almost entirely gray now. "What's new?"

"Nothing much." You shrug.

The television is going with the sound off, and his eyes wander toward it.

"Come sit down," I say. "I'm making blueberry pancakes." We all know they're your favorite.

"Really?!" You do a little hop, despite your mood. The gesture feels bittersweet. How long before you've completely outgrown these girlish leaps and jumps?

"Got any coffee?" my dad wants to know.

"Of course." I squeeze his hand in mine and feel the bones of his long fingers, his smooth olive skin.

The casement windows are halfway open and a fresh-smelling breeze blows in. Even in New York City the scent of spring is sweet. Yesterday, in the Jefferson Market Garden, I noticed a forsythia bush in full bloom; half a dozen sparrows perched on its yellow branches.

I place a pitcher of orange juice on the table, a plate of well-done bacon, the way my father likes it, low-fat milk for my mother, steaming mugs of French roast coffee. In the kitchen, I pour the batter, full of blueberries, into a hot frying pan as my mother watches from the doorway. She tells me she's been writing a poem every morning, a haiku. We listen to my father ask about your plans for the future and to your responses, so mature and well spoken. You're thinking about going to medical school, you say, maybe Stanford or Harvard, although you'd also like to travel for a while before college. Hearing you speak of your dreams and plans makes me miss you already, as if I've been projected into some future year, when you'll live in a foreign country, visit at Christmastime, and only call on my birthday.

When we sit down to eat, it's my turn to answer questions. "How's the real estate going?" my father asks.

"It's going okay," I say.

"You making any money?"

I tell him that I'm doing all right. He knows that much already because I haven't asked them for any help lately.

In the original 1997, he says to me: "If you were working this hard at almost any other profession, you'd probably be head of the company by now." But that's when I was making my living as a musician. Now there is no reason to suspect that I would ever be head of a company.

After brunch, you and your grandmother play a game of Scrabble. Your grandfather turns the volume up on the TV. The Yankees are playing one of the first games of the season. He takes a seat in the secondhand leather armchair that Alan and I recently dragged back from the flea market. It's the only piece of furniture I've ever owned that my father finds comfortable, and as he leans back into it, I feel glad to have pleased him.

I wander outside to the terrace, to see if anything green is sprouting. I've planted tulip bulbs along with a few daffodils in the pots along the brick wall. The daffodils are up and have already started to open. It's still cold enough to see my breath, but I lift my face toward the sun to feel the promise of its warmth.

Sixty-two

Harry Garfield's office is in a sparkling building near Rockefeller Center. Everything is glass and marble; even the reception area is posh. I look through a window at the pretty receptionist with the Brooklyn accent. It's been fifteen minutes since she told me Mr. Garfield would be right with me. She answers the phone every three or four seconds, puts one call on hold to take another. Church Records shares offices with a group of entertainment lawyers, and the name she recites again and again is a mouthful, but she never slips up.

Another fifteen minutes go by. Between calls, she checks her manicured nails and gives me a smile of apology. She looks as relieved as I do when a door opens and a smartly dressed blond woman says my name.

I follow the *click, click* of her high heels down a hallway, past a row of desks behind which sit secretaries in tailored jackets or tidy sweaters. Men walk past in suits and ties. She leads me through a maze of hallways that go on and on, past cubicles with ergonomic chairs, filing cabinets, and fluorescent lights, the hum of business getting done. I follow her through another doorway. "Almost there," she says. There's no way I'm going to be able to find my way back to the elevators.

In Harry's office, the walls are covered with framed rock-and-roll posters, gold records, a black-and-white photograph of the Brooklyn Bridge, and others of himself, smiling alongside various music business luminaries. The bookshelves are packed full of CDs, books, cassettes, and LPs. Harry's desk overflows with paper, in folders and in piles, more CDs, most out of their cases, pens, paper clips and rubber bands, a few pairs of sunglasses, and a jar of jelly beans.

He looks up but stays seated. "Hi, Lisa. You look great. Thanks for coming in. Have a seat."

I thank him and relax a little. I've got a T-shirt on and a jean jacket over it, tight black pants, and a pair of Doc Martens boots. My hair is messy in a good way, and I'm wearing just enough makeup to make it look as if I don't have any on. I'm going for hip, casual, and pretty.

Harry has asked me to bring any music I've got to play

for him, so I've brought the well-recorded demos made with Corbin years ago at Silver Sound, although some of those songs are not my best. I've also got a tape of a few newer, better songs, recorded on a four-track in my apartment, but those kind of sound like I'm singing underwater.

"What do you have for me?" Harry asks, rubbing his hands together.

I rummage through my big bag, trying to decide which of the two tapes to give him first, and hand him the cassette of the homemade demos. At the last second, I change my mind. "Wait, listen to this one first. Track three."

"Still True" still sounds pretty good to me. It's the strongest of my older songs. We sit in silence while it plays. He closes his eyes and nods his head. I can tell by the way he's listening that it's a good one to have started with. Three minutes and forty-something seconds go by.

"Nice tune," he says when it's done.

"Thanks." I'm playing with a rubber band I've taken from the edge of his desk, twisting it around my wrist and fingers.

"I don't remember it from the other night."

"No, it's an older song," I explain. "I try to play new stuff at the open mic."

"Pretty. I like it. What else you got?"

I hand him the other tape. He puts it into the cassette deck and presses play. The murkiness of the recording is a shock after the pristine sound of the first demo and I can tell he's confused. He listens for a couple of minutes and then shuts it off.

"You're a real talent," he says. "No doubt about that. The question is what to do with you."

I don't know what that means, but it doesn't sound good. Harry talks about himself for a while and then plays me a song by a singer he says he discovered last year. I nod my head and pretend to like it.

Before we say good-bye, he gives me a tour of the office, introduces me to the hip, young people who work there, and fills my bag with CDs of all the new Church Records releases.

Outside his door, he shakes my hand. "Stay in touch," he says. "Let me know when you're playing next."

"I will," I say, but life gets busy, and I never contact him again.

Sixty-three

When Jill Woo comes to the apartment, I attempt to give her the benefit of the doubt, but it isn't easy. She's tall, taller than I am, with flawless skin and symmetrical features. Her long black hair sways back and forth as she crosses the room.

"Hi, Ms. Nelson," she says to me, and I notice how poised she is, how careful and precise her diction. Not a passionate girl, this one. She won't be carried away by love.

Still, in the year since I caught the two of you in bed, things seem to have progressed between you. At fifteen, you're in love for the first time and speak of Jill with every sentence. She seems to be willing to go along with it at least.

"Jill is *so* smart."

"Jill is *such* a great basketball player."

"Jill's going to be in *Seventeen* magazine!"

You refer to her as your girlfriend, though I have my doubts as to whether she'd do the same. I can see the way she keeps her options open. She's like the boys I used to choose, basking in your adoration but turning away from you as you lie on the floor in front of the TV. I come in with a bowl of popcorn and see you stroke her arm. It's always you doing the reaching, while Jill leans back and coolly receives. She teases you for wearing your jeans too often. She tells you you should cut your beautiful hair. She pinches your skin at the waist. "Spare tire," she says, laughing, so you refuse to eat the fattening desserts you love.

But one day, you come home from school and throw your book bag onto the table. "I broke up with Jill," you say.

"What happened?" I ask from the kitchen where I'm unpacking groceries. I try to hide my relief.

"We've been fighting a lot."

"You want a cup of tea?"

"Sure," you say.

So I make us some tea and join you at the table. "How are you feeling?" I ask.

You look so serious and lovely, Minnow. Your nutty-brown hair falling in waves past your shoulders. You wear a crisp, white shirt, a navy A-line skirt, and heavy black shoes.

"I feel okay." I watch you spoon three heaping sugars into your tea. "I felt a little dizzy at first, and my stomach hurt, but then I was kind of relieved."

"Yeah?"

"Uh-huh, because sometimes it was exhausting, trying to be good enough for her."

"You're *too* good for her," I can't help myself from saying.

"Of course you think that. You're my mother. But with Jill, everything always has to be *so* perfect, and I'm not like that. I like to relax."

I can't help but smile at this, my relaxed, superachiever, A-student daughter.

A few days later, Gabriel calls to say he's finally making good on his threat. He plans to run for political office in the fall. He asks me how I'd feel about your spending the summer with him, in his country, to help work on his campaign. "It would be very interesting for her," your father says. "To learn about the political process, to find out Greenwich Village is not the center of the world."

"What about your family?" I ask. "Does your mother even know about her?"

"Of course she does!" He's offended. "Everyone is dying to meet her. She'll have the time of her life."

I think about my own trip to Gabriel's country, in the early eighties. Gabriel and I had been together for a year or so. He'd told me all about his beloved country, about the mountains of Terra Azul, where you can see two oceans from one patch of grass.

When we first arrived at the airport, your father ran ahead, leaving me to trail behind with our bags. I was alone going through customs when the immigration officers confiscated my passport, looking for a bribe. They were embarrassed when they found out I was with Gabriel, but they kept it just the same. Your father told me not to worry about it, and we left for our hotel. Later, he called the office of the president and explained what had happened. My passport mysteriously appeared at the front desk the next day.

Would I sleep a single night if I gave you permission to spend the summer with Gabriel in his country? "Let me get back to you," I say now. "I need to talk to her, see what she wants to do, and I really need to think about it."

"Okay," he says. "But think fast. Tell Minnow I'll speak to her on Friday."

"I will."

Sixty-four

"Mom," you say. "What do you think about *true love*?"

I'm deep into a beautiful story by Alice Munro and reluctantly put the book aside. "True love? I'm not sure what you're asking, honey."

"Well, do you think that there is just one person that, you know, you're *meant* to be with?"

"I don't believe that, no," I say.

"But I've heard you say that Gabriel is the only man *you've* ever really loved," you say.

It probably *is* what I believe, mistakenly, for myself. Even so, I have no doubt that you will love again. You're asking me, of course, because your heart is hurting. The pain of ending a relationship is tricky, Minnow. It comes in waves. It's going to get worse before it gets better.

"I think if there *is* such a thing as true love, then being with that person would allow you to relax and be yourself," I tell you. "Your true love would never ask you to become someone different from who you are."

You're a smart girl and this makes sense to you. It doesn't take away the hurt, but I can see it gives you hope.

That's when it occurs to me that a change of scenery will do you good. When I tell you about Gabriel's invitation, it lifts your spirits instantly. "Can I call him right now?" you ask excitedly.

"Go ahead," I say, trying to allow the prospect of your happiness to outweigh my fears. After you tell him, you hand the phone to me. "You'd better take good care of my girl," I say to Gabriel.

"Don't *worry*," he says, as if my worrying is only a nuisance.

Sixty-five

Gabriel makes all the arrangements for your trip. He sends you a thousand dollars to buy a suitcase and some new clothes. We go shopping at Macy's without once having to worry about what everything costs. There's no time to send away for your passport, so we take the plane ticket downtown to the passport office and they put a rush on it.

On the day of the trip, you're too excited to sit still and pace back and forth from window to window. I place my hands on your shoulders to steady you, and we both breath a deep sigh. We're to meet him at JFK, where the two of you will fly together to Gabriel's country. I think about the first time I ever traveled internationally, also with your father. I remember sitting beside him on the plane to Athens. His ease and confidence were a comfort to me. I slept most of the way with my face buried against his chest. I felt like a child but he seemed like a man.

We hail a taxi on Sixth Avenue and, in just a few minutes, are on the FDR, heading out of town. Through the window I can see the ferries and tugboats on the East River, the buildings of Long Island City.

"What if it's weird, Mom?" you ask. "I've never spent a whole summer with him before. What if I get scared?"

"If it gets weird, or you get scared, or you don't want to be there for any reason, you can come home."

"It might be a lot of fun, though," you say. "Gabriel said I could go horseback riding, and working on his campaign is going to be cool."

I'm more nervous than you are, so I try not to say too much. You've always loved meeting people, found them interesting

and easy to talk to. You're fearless about new situations. I'm
the one who's too often afraid. I look away from you so you
won't see my eyes fill with tears. I feel like I'm handing you
off to him so he can open the world up to you.

The taxi speeds along, going seventy miles per hour, and
I send up a prayer for a traffic jam to slow us down. It's all
going too fast. Time seems to be accelerating, rushing ahead,
moving faster and faster. I want to stop it now, to roll it backward. I want to hold the baby you were in my arms, to feel
your soft cheek against my lips, to see you raise yourself on
chubby legs, to hear you learn to speak. I want to put off the
moment, fast approaching, when we're going to have to say
good-bye.

Sixty-six

There's a heat wave that summer that seems to go on and on.
The air feels liquid. It's uncomfortable to breathe. I wake up
in the morning, feed the cat, the fish, and the guinea pigs,
make the bed, and put on water for coffee. The quiet of being
alone doesn't bother me. It's just strange, at first, not to hear
you in the shower, rushing around to get ready, talking on the
phone. In fifteen years we've never been apart longer than the
ten days I opened for Charlotte Winter.

When I'm not working, I sit on the terrace and play the
guitar, or fill the hours cleaning out closets and organizing
cupboards. I wash the windows and the floors with white vinegar and hot water, the way Maria once taught me. I think of

her whenever I do housework. I hear her accented voice saying, "Now, *she* knows how to clean."

Maria and Hector are living in a town called Shirley, now, on eastern Long Island, close to her son and his family. She hasn't recovered from her stroke the way her doctor said she might. It's been a long time since I've seen her, but she is often on my mind.

Outside, I hear the roar of a motorcycle and look down to the street to see Carl waving up at me from his bike. My boyfriend, that summer, is a twenty-two-year-old, Harley-riding, English busboy, a beautiful lad I met at a bar, out for a drink one night with the girls from my office.

"Hi," I call to him through the window. The heat is so thick that it wiggles the air. "Want to come up?"

"Come for a ride," he calls, and holds out the helmet he's brought for me. I'm afraid of motorcycles, but tell him I'll throw on a pair of jeans and be right down.

Gracefully, we weave through traffic, the eyes of drivers and pedestrians upon us. Carl is the sort you trust at the wheel. He can build an engine from a pile of nuts and bolts. He's also good with a pool cue. I hold on to him and feel the oblique muscles along his sides, the bones of his back and rib cage. He's tall and lean, with curly reddish hair already beginning to thin at the crown. His skin is white and softly freckled. He thinks he's in love with me.

We don't speak as the wind whistles through our helmets. There's no way to hear a thing over the roar of the Harley. But even later, on the quiet City Island dock, which is where he takes me, our attempts at conversation seem to miss. He's just a boy, and I don't give him half a chance. He's someone to have fun with, to sleep with, but too willing and gentle to be more.

He pours some water, from a plastic bottle in his backpack, onto a handkerchief, and presses it against my neck, shoulders, face, and chest. Even the breeze off the Hudson River feels hot as breath.

His lips are full and soft beneath my own. His tongue darts in and out. "You make me so horny," he says.

"Don't say that," I scold him. "It makes you sound fourteen."

"Oh, pardon me, Grandma," he says, unhooking my bra with one hand and cupping my breast with the other.

Marry him, the breeze whispers. But I break his heart instead.

Many years later, when the Internet is reconnecting every old lover and classmate, I get an e-mail from Carl. He's become a professional kickboxer in Thailand, he writes. I can still feel his wound in the way he phrases the greeting, as if offering up his throat to be cut or kissed.

He pushes me back on the hard dock now, licks my breasts, and gently blows on my nipples. "How does that feel?"

"Don't ask," I say. "Just do it."

He undoes his pants and pushes his way inside me, roughly, the way I like it. He'd prefer to be gentle, to whisper tender words, but he wants to please me. The moment of penetration, of being entered, is like forgetting. It always takes me by surprise.

Later, we go to an East Village bar full of restaurant workers and English boys. He challenges one to a game of pool. We drink a couple of shots, a pitcher of beer, and then another round. Too drunk to walk, I attempt to crawl to the restroom on my hands and knees. Carl pulls me to my feet, laughing. He can hold his liquor. He reaches into the pockets of my jeans looking for another twenty.

"Wait." My words slur. "I think I need to go home."

"Just one more," says Carl. He holds me upright with one arm and opens the ladies' room door with the other.

In the morning the phone rings ten times before it wakes me. My head is splitting, my mouth full of cotton. The night before is a mixed-up blur. I have a vague memory of pushing Carl out the door while he begged me to stay. "Food poisoning," I tell Arnie, my boss. He's called to ask where the hell I am. My ten o'clock is waiting.

My hangover feels like the flu, and I'm sick for a day and a half, but by the weekend Carl is outside, calling up to me, and we do the whole thing again. We do it so often that summer; it becomes routine.

Sixty-seven

Every day when I get home, I listen for the sound of your voice on the answering machine. I play your messages over and over. Finally, a letter arrives from you, just after the Fourth of July.

Dear Mom,

How are you?

Today we visited Coiba, an island that once was a prison for politicos, but now is known for its luxury resort. The prison is still here although there aren't many prisoners left. They sweep the beach for the tourists.

I'm having a wonderful time. Mi abuela, Nora, is very funny. Even though she's divorced from Gabriel Sr., she keeps a chair for him at the table. He comes

*to dinner almost every night. He likes to tell outland-
ish stories. Gabriel says not to believe a word he says.
I have so many relatives here, aunts and uncles and
cousins. Many of them have the same names, which is
confusing! They all talk and ask questions at the same
time, but my Spanish is getting better! Maria would be
very proud of me.*

*Everywhere we go it's like being in a parade. People
surround Gabriel and want to shake his hand. He stops
and talks to every one of them, old man, housewife, or
pretty girl. He never gets tired of it. There's a lot of excitement about the election, and I think he's going to win.*

*How are Tiger, Z, Cinnamon, and Goldy? I miss
you all very much.*

*Love & xoxoxoxoxox,
Minnow*

Sixty-eight

"Your daughter is a lesbian," Gabriel says. He's called before
nine in the morning.

"Yeah, so what?" I'm hungover and in no mood for his crap.

"So what is, let's hope the newspapers don't get ahold of it.
Illegitimate, lesbian daughter of candidate Gabriel Luna!"

"Oh, relax," I tell him. "How did you find out, anyway?"

"She told me," he says. "I told her she was too young to
know *what* she is. I told her it was *your* fault. I think you
raised her to be a man-hater." He starts to lecture me about
his mother and grandmother, who were good role models and

made him the man he is today. I'm too tired to argue, and he can feel it. He's called looking for a fight and is disappointed. "Hey, what's wrong with *you*? You sound like the living dead."

Without you, Minnow, I've lost my bearings. I'm rudderless in high winds, adrift at sea, shipwrecked on a lonely island.

On a Saturday evening, I follow behind a family on Sixth Avenue, two parents and three children. The husband and wife hold hands. The kids race one another to the corner. As I watch them, it strikes me that this is the real treasure of life, walking home with your own family on a summer night.

Approaching the apartment, I see Carl waiting for me with a six-pack of Guinness under his arm. He stands back while I open the door and follows me upstairs. How strange it is, I think, to be spending my days and nights with strangers: real estate clients and a boy too young to understand anything. Why haven't I made a safe nest for us the way everyone else seems to? Even Alan, my faithful holdout, has plans to marry his girlfriend in the spring.

Carl and I drink the Guinness until it's gone. "Want to shoot some pool?" he asks.

"Sure," I say, and so we head over to the East Village bar.

There are so many nights like this, they blend into one. A hot summer hallucination of Harley rides, playing pool, and making love on sweat-soaked sheets, stinking of alcohol.

Late that summer, a girl at the office talks me into going to an AA meeting, and I follow her down two flights of stairs into a large basement under a Gothic church in SoHo. I spot Charlotte Winter sitting in the front row, in a room of about a hundred people. She waves and signals for me to take the seat beside her, so I do. I scan her expression to see if she's making fun of me, or if there's any condescension or malice in her smile, but she seems to be genuinely glad to see me.

At the head of the room, there's a long table, with a folding chair behind it. A man speaks into a microphone. "Testing, testing," he says. "Can you hear me?"

There's joviality in the rush of responses.

"Yup."

"Yeah."

"Uh-huh, we can hear you."

"Loud and clear."

These people can't be alcoholics, I think to myself. They're too happy.

A speaker is introduced and proceeds to tell a story. I've never heard anything so honest in my life. He doesn't hide the ugly parts, the way I've always thought you had to. He talks about how from the time he was a kid he always felt uncomfortable in his own skin. He describes getting into a car accident that put his best friend in a coma. He says he was a disappointment to everyone who loved him, and that everything he tried to do failed, or fell apart. But since he stopped drinking all that has changed.

"AA has given me a new life," he says.

I don't know if I have a drinking problem, but I like being in that room. I want to hear other stories. I have the sense that belonging to AA may help tether me to the world, and I'm desperate to be thrown a rope that summer. It seems like a long time since I've had anything to hold on to.

So I get sober. I break it off with Carl, and Charlotte becomes my sponsor. I tell her that I think I drink so much because I miss you, but she says that that's just an excuse and the reason I drink so much is because I'm an alcoholic.

When you get home at the end of the summer, I take you with me to a meeting.

"I'm proud of you, Mom," you say.

Sixty-nine

In the original 1998, I've been sober for about three years by this time. I've been coming to meetings, off and on, since the mid-eighties.

I walk up to the wooden podium at my favorite Chelsea meeting, adjust the microphone, and introduce myself to the group as an alcoholic.

"Hi, Lisa," they say, all together.

The room is full of AA members I've come to know, some to love. Most of these people have heard part, or all, of my story before.

I'm tired, just back from another quick trip to Los Angeles, where I met with an agent who has agreed to represent me as a composer. Soon I'll settle there, leave New York for good. But this evening I'm glad to be back among friends.

I tell the group that I first came to AA, many years ago, not because I thought I was an alcoholic but because I was heart-broken and desperate and couldn't stop myself from doing stupid, irresponsible things. I always think of Gabriel when I tell this part. I'll never forget how much it hurt to lose him, as if I'd been thrown back into a cold universe, my chance at happiness gone.

I say that drinking was my medicine, until it stopped work-ing. Without it, I was lonely and uptight and a bitch. I couldn't imagine surviving without something to numb myself.

But I've learned to accept that this is what it feels like to be a human being: happy, or lonely, or sad, or afraid; to go on living when things are hard, or scary good, or just kind of in the middle; to roll with life's disappointments.

When I speak of disappointment, I feel the shadow of you,

Minnow, though I keep you pretty well hidden from myself, buried deep. You are a part of the past that I don't allow myself to dwell on.

I wrap things up with a few words about my career. It makes me feel better and gives my AA story a happy ending. The group applauds as I take my seat. We go to a secretary's break before resuming with a show of hands.

Seventy

Gabriel loses the election in November.

"I'm pretty sure it was fixed," he says. "But we're not going to ask for a recount. It's disappointing. Still, the numbers show there *are* people who want change, and I'm proud to be a part of it."

"I so admire you for trying," I tell him.

"Gracias, mi amor," he says. "I appreciate it."

After the election, Gabriel goes back to L.A. His new record wins a Grammy. He gets a supporting role in a movie directed by Clint Eastwood. In 2002, he returns to his country to run again, this time for a more modest position, and wins by a landslide.

When Gabriel and I were young, he once told me that he was different from other people. "They think because they hold a fork like I do that they're the same as me. Not all people are created equal, Lisa. That's a lie."

Seventy-one

"I'm never going to have children," you say, pushing your arugula around with a fork. We're at the French bistro across the street. You've decided it's a contradiction to love animals and eat meat, and have declared yourself a vegetarian. You haven't figured out what's okay to eat yet, though, so have ordered only a green salad. I take a bite of my turkey club, hoping to tempt you. You reach across for my french fries and devour them one by one. "You probably would have been a famous musician if you didn't have me."

"Probably not. And where would *you* be? Besides, I don't think being famous is what it's cracked up to be."

"Gabriel says it gives you a platform to help others. Plus, it makes you rich."

"Being rich doesn't necessarily make you happy," I say, signaling our waitress for more coffee.

"Gabriel says that's just what rich people tell poor people to keep them quiet."

"Oh, does he? Well, Gabriel doesn't know everything."

"Anyway, there are too many people in the world already." You're at the age when young people discover the world is broken and jump to hasty and idealistic conclusions. And, of course, you probably will have children, Minnow. Most people do.

After lunch, we walk arm in arm back to the apartment. The song I'm working on has a pretty melody that gets stuck in my head. Its lyric sings:

Good-bye, good-bye,
Good-bye.

You're a freshman at Northeastern University in Boston. You come home every other weekend at first. I meet your train at the station and see you from far away, smiling, dragging ten pounds of dirty laundry behind you, hair knotted into dreadlocks, wearing worn overalls with a hole in the knee.

At the end of the weekend, I help carry your bags back to Penn Station. We load them onto the train. When I lift your backpack to the overhead rack, you pull it down again to remove a book or a sweater. "Go, Mom," you say, worried that I intend to ride with you all the way back to Boston.

Little by little, you'll break away, fall in love again, spend a summer in Costa Rica, and decide you never want to come back.

With only moments to spare, I step off the train and stand waving to you from the platform. Through the darkened window I watch the shape of you becoming smaller and smaller as the train pulls slowly out of the station.

Part 3

The Original 2010

Seventy-two

All the way from JFK, I watch the skyline in the distance. It's always bittersweet to come back. When my father was sick, I lived at The Surrey, near Lenox Hill Hospital, for almost a month, shared a room with my mother. For weeks, we sat at his bedside, my mother, my sister, and I, waiting for test results, questioning doctors, coaxing him to eat something, while he looked less and less like himself. Until finally, he was released to hospice care, and then he was gone.

I've been back a number of times since his death, for holiday visits with my family, or an occasion with Alan and his. Last year, we all gathered at the cemetery to see my father's headstone unveiled.

Usually, as soon as I could, I returned to my life in Los Angeles. But I've left my car in the long-term lot this time. All that relentless sunshine can be depressing when you're already depressed.

"You need to just *move*," Jules said. "Take a trip! Go to Europe." Or New York, I thought. It occurred to me that Marta Lightman lived somewhere in the tristate area. I had just agreed to work on her score.

Traffic slows to a standstill approaching the Midtown Tunnel, and I curse myself for forgetting to tell the driver to take the Triborough. Not yet arrived and already reverting to New York ways. I shift and sigh while he pretends not to notice.

Eventually, we're through and on the other side. "It's okay I take First Avenue?" he asks.

"Maybe the FDR would be faster," I say, leaning toward him. There's Plexiglas between us. I notice his ID photo. I think he's from Ghana, or someplace else in West Africa.

"Okay," he says, and soon we're speeding uptown along the East River.

It's spring again in New York City. The earthy scent of it blows through the half-open taxi windows as we cut through Central Park at Ninety-seventh Street. The apple blossom trees are in bloom. It's the best time of year to be here, if you don't count the fall, when the leaves are turning. My eyes drink up the architecture, fashionable pedestrians, the tended trees of Central Park West, the museum, the elegant buildings on West Eighty-first Street. Then we make the left onto Columbus.

Though the Café Miriam is now a Mexican restaurant with a different name, the sidewalks surrounding the Museum of Natural History are still made of cobblestone. Columbus Avenue is more crowded than ever with restaurants, shops, and bars. As we pass the Sheridan, the third-floor windows seem to call out to me. I half expect to see Gabriel's head pop out, and behind him the girl I was, worried and young. She'd have given anything to know what the future held. What would she make of herself, thirty years later?

I think about something the record producer Will Dimitri once said to me. We were at a bar in Chelsea, and I was still drinking, or maybe I was drinking again, because there have been times when I struggled with sobriety. It was a long time ago.

"Will," I asked, "why do you think we have the lives we do?"

He was very smart, drunk or sober. "Your life is just an extension of what you are," he said. "It's an illusion, this idea that we *choose* our lives. You *are* your life and there's not much you can do about it."

We come to a halt outside Alan's building, a limestone prewar on West End Avenue, and I pay the taxi driver from Ghana. I'll spend the night here until my sublet begins tomorrow. I remove my keyboard and a suitcase from the trunk. Years of touring have made me an efficient traveler. Rarely do I need more than a single bag. Again, I think of Gabriel. He's the one who taught me, a million years ago: "You bring it, you carry it."

I lean on the buzzer and hear the cacophony of children screaming and the dog barking as Alan says, "Come on up!"

Seventy-three

Once again I am his sous chef, chopping onions, mushrooms, and green peppers. He watches over my shoulder, says, "A little finer," and I make the correction without comment. Alan's gray hair reaches almost to his shoulders. He looks good. Happiness suits him.

Maeve is working late. She's a poet, but also has a real job—one with a paycheck, which allows them to live well. Alan's job has been mainly playing the guitar with me, but he's got a regular Saturday-night gig now and says he's picked up some other work, too.

I'm not performing anymore. It hit me one day that I was holding on to something that no longer made sense. I walked off the stage at the end of another tour, turned to Alan, and said, "That's it. I'm done." He didn't believe me. I don't think he believes it, one hundred percent, even now. It doesn't mean I've stopped doing what I love. That's what I tell him. I've just had to find other ways. That's all.

Justin and Samantha, Alan's six-year-old twins, sit coloring at the kitchen table. He separates them when the hitting starts.

"She's bossy," Justin says to me about his sister, "and she pinches."

"He started it," she says.

"Nobody's pinching anybody," Alan says calmly.

I sit down at the table, between them, and begin to draw. I don't know how to talk to kids, but can usually get around it by joining them in creative activities. When I pick up a gold glitter pen, Samantha takes an interest. She snatches it from me to add her own gold glitter. She has Maeve's wild red hair. Justin looks exactly like Alan and Alan's parents.

By the time Maeve gets home, dinner is almost ready, and the kids and I are Wii bowling. Lola the beagle is the first to welcome her.

Maeve has a pretty Irish face, freckles, and an upturned nose.

"Hi, Mommy," the kids say.

"Hi, guys." She kisses my cheek. "How are you, Lisa? Good to see you. Thanks for keeping them entertained."

Maeve saves her warmest greeting for Alan. I see their kiss out of the corner of my eye. The kids have gone back to the game and are arguing over whose turn it is.

"Mommy!" Justin says. "Tell Samantha to stop."

"Play nice, Samantha."

"I didn't do anything!"

"Five minutes till dinner, everybody," Alan says.

Loneliness is like being inside your own bubble.

Seventy-four

The brownstone off Lexington on the north side of Ninety-
first Street has a worn facade and an ancient fire escape, but
its oversize front door, painted matte black, gives it a certain elegance. Inside, there's a curved banister and a carpeted
stairway that leads to the apartment—a narrow floor-through,
three flights up. It has a tiny foyer, a hallway to the right,
leading to the bathroom and kitchen. On the left, there's an
archway you pass through to the living room, which is small
but has high ceilings and a fireplace. Off the living room is the
bedroom, big enough only for the full-size bed it contains, but
that's fine with me. I don't expect to be sharing it.

The place is sparsely furnished in the way of short-term
rentals. It has the basics: a sofa, a table, two chairs, and a TV.
Everything is dated but clean. I unpack my own pillow and
make the bed. Place a plain glass vase of yellow tulips on the
fireplace mantel, put the rest of my things away.

My first night in the apartment, unable to sleep, I lie awake
listening to the traffic on Third Avenue. Through an open
window, I can hear a group of young people go by, laughing
and singing. A dog starts to bark. I find myself thinking about
the last time I had sex—more than a year ago. As the man I
loved reached for me, the feeling I had was one of relief. We'd
been fighting all day, but maybe we'd get through it. I felt
love, sadness, longing, defeat, desire, need, as I kissed his face
and ran my hands over the rough growth of his nearly shaved
head. He was a big man with a broad back. I could barely get
my arms around his body, heavy over mine.

What if it was the last time I'll ever be with someone I love?
My mind begins to race through every regret and fear I have,

every slight and resentment. Monkey mind, it's called in Buddhism.

I've been learning to meditate this year and attempt it, breathing deeply and counting my breaths. I keep breathing and counting, and after a few minutes, I find I'm able to slow my thoughts down until finally they do stop coming, and it's almost like floating in space. I feel very relaxed then and seem to be drifting off to sleep, when another thought breaks through to the surface. Somewhere I've read that human beings aren't any good at predicting their own happiness. We are incapable of rightly knowing what will make us happy.

That's the nature of my problem, I think. I've made choices that can never be rectified. I turn my pillow over to the cool side and roll onto my back. But there's no cure for my monkey mind that night.

At some point, I know I do fall asleep, because when I wake up it's almost noon, and I stumble into the kitchen, thankful for the drip coffeemaker I find there.

Seventy-five

Pushed up against the living room window, the table becomes my desk. It gives me a familiar view of rooftops and sky. Thirty years ago, I lived in another brownstone just twenty blocks from here.

I turn my computer on, check e-mail, and read the paper. Finally I reach for a manila envelope in my bag. Finding the DVD inside, I slip it into the disk drive of my laptop.

I Gave My Love is a documentary about a young single mother in a depressed Catskill Mountain town. I'm to meet with Marta Lightman, its director, later in the week and hope to have a better idea of what I'm doing by then.

In the opening scene, the camera follows a nurse into a bright hospital room where a young woman, Ashley, is screaming and crying as she gives birth to a daughter. Ashley is pretty and blond, even as she grows red-faced, her hair soaked in sweat. She's screaming, "Oh, *shit*! Oh, my fuckin' *God*!"

My song "Don't Fall In" is playing in the background. Marta has filled her temp-score with songs from my second record, *Room Inside,* a collection of folk rock and ballads that *Rolling Stone* gave three and a half stars in 1992. I'm to replace all the music with a new score.

After her baby's birth, Ashley is abandoned by her abusive boyfriend, moves back in with her crack-addicted mother, loses her job at Dunkin' Donuts, fills out forms for public assistance. In the final scene, the baby's first birthday is being celebrated in her grandmother's double-wide with an angel food cake and a few unwholesome-looking relatives. She grins happily, her face and hands covered in cake.

"Still True" plays through the scene. Its lyric, written so long ago for Gabriel, is now a love song to a child.

> *Baby, all I've ever looked for is a safe place,*
> *All I've ever longed for is your warm embrace . . .*

The most moving scenes in the film are the ones between Ashley and her newborn. In one, she breast-feeds her daughter while being interviewed. "What does it feel like?" the unseen interviewer asks.

"I can't describe it," whispers Ashley. The way she says it tells you everything. The best part is when the baby reaches up to hold a piece of her mother's hair. Such a touching, intimate gesture. It's like a knife to the heart every time.

Seventy-six

By early afternoon, the sun is reflecting so brightly off the windows across the street, I decide to go for a run. Outside, the air is almost balmy, one of those spring days that feel more like summer. A young couple ducks past me on the sidewalk. I see them nuzzle like colts and remember, instantly, what that felt like.

Looking toward Central Park in the distance, I try to pace myself. Lately, I tend to get overheated and can't cool down. The hypothalamus gland is located at the base of the brain. It regulates body temperature and ceases to work properly after menopause. I know this because I've googled my symptoms. Unfortunately, aging is not a problem that can be solved with a little exercise or Botox.

I jog past the brick and limestone buildings on East Ninetieth Street on my way to the park entrance at Fifth Avenue, where curved staircases lead to the Jacqueline Kennedy Onassis Reservoir. On opposite corners stand two very grand buildings: the Cooper-Hewitt Museum and the Church of Heavenly Rest. It's one of the loveliest spots in the entire city.

Over the last ten years, the city seems to have undergone a transformation, too. Maybe only my perspective has changed,

but it now appears to be overrun with young families. Baby
carriages, pregnant women in tight T-shirts, bellies round and
proud; men wearing baby harnesses; mothers and fathers still
in their early thirties with toddlers and infants on every arm,
hand, and shoulder. I'm pretty sure it wasn't always this way.

The ache that lodges itself between my shoulder blades and
beneath my rib cage struggles to accept things as they are.
That's what middle age is all about, acceptance and regret.
The realization that you're no longer young comes smack up
against the recognition that, soon enough, you will be old.
What will it be like to have the world shift out from under you,
to live in a failing body but still feel like a shiny bird inside?

I think of my father then, as I often do. I want to remember him as a robust man of sixty, but sometimes his final face
creeps in like a bad dream. He knew the answer to everything.
How did he do that? From tectonic plates, to algebra, to who
the movie stars were dating. I can still conjure the sound of
his voice saying my name.

After he died, my mother seemed stunned and confused for
a while, as if she'd left him somewhere and needed to go find
him. But amazingly, she's made a new life for herself. I can
barely keep up with her descriptions of bingo and bridge and
movie nights. She's going to Israel with her widows' group in
the fall.

I veer off the bridle path, over a hill, past the tennis courts,
and pick up a dirt road that runs along the Park Drive going
south. Everywhere others are enjoying the warm day. Runners
and cyclists, students, squirrels and birds, dogs rolling in the
grass. It's hard not to feel a part of it all.

Approaching the Sheep Meadow, I come upon a television
crew. A girl is being interviewed with the green field behind

her. Evidently, she's to give a concert as part of the Summer-
Stage series. She has long, dirty-blond hair, parted in the
middle, and wears too much makeup for the bright afternoon.
I can feel her confidence radiating. Others stop to listen, too.
She's at the height of it, or nearly so.

"I don't want to be another guitar girl," I hear her say, in
explanation for why she plays the ukelele. It makes me smile.
I was once a version of that girl, I think, and Jules was, too,
just a few years before me. There's always a girl starting out:
a musician, or actress, or dancer, who believes she is special,
that her youth, or beauty, is not the reason. But the world is
just as happy with the next girl, and there's always another
girl waiting to step into the temporary light.

I'll tell Jules, I think. It will remind her of the summer she
played Ophelia. A prestigious Shakespeare in the Park produc-
tion, at the start of her career. "That was such a good time for
me," she always says. "Remember?"

I stumble upon *Conspiracy* sometimes flipping through
channels late at night. It always takes me by surprise to see
her fine young face. What is Jules doing right now? I wonder.
Pulling her cart along Venice Beach?

Sometimes you see people you used to know when they
were young, and they look like they're wearing an "old" suit,
a Halloween costume of fat and wrinkles. You can still see
the person beneath, but barely. Jules is the opposite of those
people. Time has concentrated her. Dressed in bright vintage
sweaters and jeans, her hair dyed a version of the old yellow-
blond, she's well known at the thrift stores and junkyards in
Santa Monica and Venice, where she finds metal wire, dresses
with crinolines, doll parts, shoes, and other things for her
artwork. She lugs it all back to her studio in a fold-up cart,

which gives her the look of what we used to call a bag lady. But she either doesn't know or doesn't care. Holding her cigarette between thumb and forefinger, paint or plaster beneath short fingernails, she squints one eye as she brings it to her lips and drags deeply. She's become a character she'd have loved to play in her acting days.

Last week, we stood together in her yard as she fed acorns and walnuts to the squirrels. They come right out of the trees and stand on hind legs for her like little men. She's always had a way with animals.

"See that one there? That's Charlie. He's very brave."

I noticed she was covering her mouth with her hand. "What's going on with your face?" I asked.

"Oh, I broke another damn tooth," she said. "Pain in the ass. Next life, I want to come back with good teeth!"

"I'm coming back as a bird," I told her.

"An old turkey?" she joked, and we laughed.

"Maybe a sparrow," I said, thinking of the way they gather in spring.

"Nice," she said, but later she sent me a clip of a sparrow being pecked at, relentlessly, by another sparrow. In the subject line, she'd written, *Are you sure?*

Seventy-seven

On Sunday my mother takes the train in from Long Island. Climbs the three flights of stairs slowly but steadily.

"Oh, this is nice," she says, about the rental apartment. Her sunny nature, which used to drive me crazy, now seems a rare gift. She's different, too. I think it's because she doesn't have to stand by my father anymore, to translate for him and cajole him. But she says it's because they were like two parts of one organism, and now she is only half.

The restaurant we choose for our brunch of eggs Benedict and blueberry pancakes is not one he would have chosen. He'd have steered us toward the coffee shop on Ninety-sixth Street instead. We pay the expensive bill and talk about what he'd have said: "Outrageous!"

After brunch, we hail a taxi to the West Side. We're on our way to see a movie that's playing at an art-house theater across from Lincoln Center. This, too, is new. Art-house movies and brunches. It feels like his ghost is watching us in amazement. My father's absence is so pronounced, it's a presence. But we pretend to be just the two of us, doing what we want to do.

We arrive at the theater early and after buying our tickets wander into the courtyard behind Avery Fisher Hall to see what's going on. A stage has been set up there, along with about a thousand folding chairs. Security guards stand by a red velvet rope, stretched across to keep fans at bay. We have no idea what the event is or who is scheduled to perform, but it's a nice day, so we take a seat beneath a stand of trees and listen as a sound check gets under way.

From the first blast of trumpet to the unmistakable beat of the timbales, I recognize the music of my twenties. Salsa. Afro-Cuban music, it's sometimes called. I pull out my phone to research who's playing, but before my search is complete, I hear a voice speak into a microphone. "And one and two," it says, and I know.

"It's Gabriel," I say to my mother even before he starts to sing.

"How can you tell?" she asks.

"I just can." It's a surprise, even to me, that after so many years I recognize the sound of his voice from the first word. We sit under the trees and listen to his song as he stops and starts again. It's a sound check, after all. He seems frustrated. I can't be sure about what from so far away, but I figure it's probably because he can't hear himself in the monitors or is unhappy with the mix. I've been in his shoes many times. Finally, he seems satisfied, or at least has accepted the limitations of the sound system. He thanks everyone and leaves the stage.

"Are you going to say hello?" my mother asks. I can see that she wants me to. But the stage is a block away, and even if we were able to get a message to him, what would be the point? Maybe he'd come out to say hello, and then what?

"I don't want to be late for our movie," I say.

She looks disappointed, as if it's a coincidence too big to pass up, maybe even meant to be. But I steer her away.

Many years ago I went to see Gabriel play at a supper club in Midtown. I convinced Alan to come along, because I was nervous to go by myself. Seeing him perform again had been confusing and upsetting. His every mannerism was so deeply familiar to me, though I didn't really know him anymore. It struck me that I would never get over it, not the pain of losing him, or the relationship itself. The experience had left me depressed for weeks.

Life is like a big empty house when you're young, windows open wide. But over time, you close off rooms that are too painful to visit, whole wings you can't bear to enter. Eventually, you live in a book-filled kitchen off the porch, hiding from your own history.

"What?" my mother asks. I must have a faraway look in my eye.

"Oh, it's nothing," I say, leading her through the crowd.

Seventy-eight

That night, when I google Gabriel, among the many photographs I find is one I took myself, thirty years ago, on a trip to Paris. Its caption reads *Gabriel Luna by the Eiffel Tower.* Somewhere, I have one just like it of me standing in the same spot. I don't recall much about the trip, but as I look at the picture, a few things come back to me. We'd gone to Berlin first and then to Rome, where I got a haircut that made me look like a baby bird.

I drag the photo to my desktop, to inspect it more closely; it's a Polaroid, taken with my old SX-70 camera. Gabriel's hair is lifting in the breeze (when he still had hair!). As I stare at the image, the soft blue work shirt he wears becomes more familiar and then the gold cross around his neck. I remember his hands, smallish with slender fingers. Funny to find such a personal memento on the Internet. How did it get there? The thing that strikes me most about it is the love in his eyes. Eyes that were looking into mine. Gabriel had loved me on that gray day in Paris.

I don't know why it takes me so long to remember the most important thing, but suddenly I do—I'd been nauseated over breakfast in Rome, realized my breasts were swollen and my period was late. Had I told him yet, when this picture was taken? Maybe I was waiting until we were back in New York, afraid of ruining our holiday. His expression gave no clue.

In my mind, I make a revision to its caption: *Gabriel Luna by the Eiffel Tower with Child.* This is a photograph of the time when everything could have been different.

Seventy-nine

Riding the elevator up to the fourth floor, my excitement mounts. It's like time travel to come down this hallway and stand at the door of Silver Sound.

Harv has retired to Miami, and the studio has new owners and a new name. In the office, I check to see if my eight-by-ten, a Warner Bros. publicity photo, is still Scotch-taped to the wall, but of course it isn't.

I breathe in its particular scent of musty, refrigerated air. Most of the smaller recording studios are long gone, but Silver has hung on, somehow. Or Planet has. Its new name is not the only change; C is a digital room, and much of the equipment has been updated. But I'm happy to see that the Yamaha C7 still occupies a corner of room A. Once, I recorded all of my demos here, for Warner Bros. Records, and even before that, with my first band, before I had a deal.

I plan to record live drums and piano in the big room for the documentary project. It's the most fun thing in the world to record with a band in a studio like this one. At one time there was no other way. You saved up your pennies, or made a spec deal with a studio. You bought expensive two-inch tape and hired an engineer to work the Neve console. It's a way of life that has gone extinct, really, for most musicians. We'll be doing the majority of this project—overdubs and edits—at Alan's place, using Pro Tools.

Marta arrives a few minutes later. She's an elegant woman who carries a few extra pounds well. There are silver streaks in her dark hair, and she wears a crisp white tunic. As she takes my hand, I remember having heard that many years ago she lost a young child to cancer. It occurs to me that she's addressed the tragedy in every film she makes. That's what we do, as artists, I think, explore one obsessional subject. Address a specific trauma, or wound, again and again.

I show Marta around the studio and explain my idea to her. I want to hire all of the musicians who played on *Room Inside* to play on the new score. It will give the music a similar feel to that record, which I know she wants, but will also be very different. I'm not a fan of using songs as film score, I tell her. I think it turns a movie into a music video.

"What about 'Still True'?" she asks.

As a compromise, I agree to do a new version of that old song. It will be fun to revisit, and maybe I can convince her to use it only as the credits roll.

After we leave the studio, we stop for a bite to eat at a French bistro on Eleventh Street. I know the restaurant from when I lived across from it, on Sixth Avenue. We're seated at a marble table by the oak bar. I can see my old apartment through the plate glass. It looks different, because the ancient casement windows have been swapped out for ones that are probably energy-efficient.

We order lunch, and I ask about Ashley's baby, Lorelei. They're both doing well, Marta says. Ashley has a good job working for a utility company. The little girl is exceptional, bright, and cheerful. "She got the happiness gene," Marta says. "Do you have children?"

"No," I say. "No children."

Marta takes his photograph from her wallet then and places it on the table between us. Her son, Claudio, has been gone nearly twenty years, but time means nothing to grief. "I still think about him every day," she says. For a moment I think of you, Minnow. I picture you floating like a mist or a spirit.

After lunch we say our good-byes, and I wander through the Village, struck by how much it's changed. Everything has been replaced, renamed, renovated, reopened in a new location. Doorways are cleaner, or more decrepit, new windows shine over old brick. I can see the past, layered beneath the facade of storefronts, restaurants, and apartment buildings. It's like being in all of those other years at the same time.

That night, I have a dream: I'm in my house in Silver Lake, opening closets and doors into rooms that are empty. As I search the house, I grow more and more agitated. Everything is gone.

Waking from the dream, I feel disoriented and try to fall back asleep but can't. The red numbers of the bedside clock blink 5:00 A.M. It's three hours earlier in L.A. The man I loved will still be sleeping beside the woman who shares his bed now. I called him E, his first initial and also his last.

When the sky gets light, I put on my running shoes and go down to the street. The morning is cool, though it's been warm the last few days and is supposed to be again. The sun is coming up over the East River, pink and orange. A neon sign glows red beside it. Other runners are out, dog walkers, a few people just getting home from the night before. It strikes me that in the early morning, there is often this feeling of optimism. What will the day bring? It must be a tool for survival of the species, I think, programmed into our DNA. Even if your house has burned down, or you're sick, or realize your life is full of mistakes that can never be undone, still you feel it. Hope.

Eighty

Leaving Paris, Gabriel and I would have taken a car to Charles de Gaulle Airport, checked our bags. Gotten a bite to eat, and the newspaper, and boarded our flight to New York. We would have been seven hours in the air, or was it eight? Seven one way and eight the other, depending on the winds. Probably we watched a movie, had our dinner on a tray, slept beneath a thin blanket, my head resting on his shoulder.

When we landed at JFK, Gabriel would have gone straight to the head of the taxi line and gotten away with it, the way he did everything. What did we talk about all the way home? His career, most likely. It was usually that. Unless I'd behaved badly, gotten drunk or thrown a jealous tantrum. In that case, my bad behavior might be the topic.

But I can't remember any of it, in any case. When did I tell him?

I'd have been worried about my cats, having left them for so long, but would have said nothing about it. Instead, I'd have gone with him back to his apartment, unwilling, or unable, to leave his side.

What was I thinking? I can't remember it! I want to remember.

Me, pregnant with you, in 1982.

Eighty-one

Opening my eyes in New York City, I forget where I am some-times, and by that I mean not only the location but also the year. I'm time-traveling in my dreams.

For the first few minutes of consciousness, I lie awake, wait-ing to come back to myself, listening to the sound of faraway trucks and car horns, a white-noise layer behind the quiet of morning that is as still as the city ever gets.

Making coffee is a ritual, a process. Put on the water. Grind the beans. Let the French press sit for four minutes; slowly push the grounds to the bottom. The pressure sometimes causes the boiling liquid to spill over the edge. Half awake, I carry the strong-smelling brew to my desk, turn on my com-puter and keyboard, take in the view of treetops and brown-stones, and begin to work on the music for *I Gave My Love*.

Writing a song is a kind of puzzle. First comes the idea, next the form, melody, and lyric—pieces that define and shape one another.

Writing music for a movie is different. The picture provides the idea. The movement and tension of the scene suggest the form. You plug into it, absorb all of the elements, and *it* tells you what it wants.

Again and again, I run a scene: Ashley carrying the baby on a suburban street, surrounded by snowdrifts and bare trees. The wrong music can crush a moment like a petal under a boot. But when it's right, it makes you *feel* everything else, the white-winter sky, Ashley's loneliness, the curiosity in the baby's expression.

This is how my days take shape: Mornings I work on the score. In the afternoon, I run errands, or go to an AA meeting, or meet Alan for lunch. In the evening, I make dinner for myself in the kitchen and eat it in front of the TV on a chipped white plate. I watch crime dramas. The same show plays on different channels, from different years. It's strange to see the lead detective with long hair and short, at thirty and forty. Time compressed.

On the weekends, I make myself get out for a run. The park is full of children playing soccer and other games. I jog past them at my slow, steady pace. I hear their high-pitched voices, the whistles of the coaches, parents applauding from the side-lines. How has this happened? I'm on the periphery, a solitary animal in a world of connected creatures.

Eighty-two

Maeve calls to invite me for the Fourth of July weekend. She and Alan have rented a cottage in the Hamptons for the summer. "It's pretty rustic," she says, "and north of the high-way, so don't get too excited."

I know the Hamptons from family vacations, making out in the dunes with my boyfriend as a teenager. North or south doesn't matter to me. But after hours of sitting in traffic on the LIE, we make the turn onto 27, and though I recognize the flatness of the landscape and the quality of the light, I can see that the beachy villages of my youth have been replaced by rich suburban towns. Only the Candy Kitchen in Bridge-hampton looks the same. We drive around the block to find a parking spot and wait ten minutes for a booth in the back. The kids order milk shakes and french fries, but it feels more like a film set than the real thing. From across the room, we watch as a former New York City mayor is seated. A popular TV star comes in and takes a stool at the counter. We pretend to ignore them, just like everybody else.

Later that day, six-year-old Samantha tells me she's never going to get married or have children. "I'm going to live in my own apartment and have three cats," she says.

I laugh. She has no idea that it's the fate that's supposed to fill single women everywhere with dread.

We're on the beach at the end of Ocean Road and have wandered far from the crowd and our blanket. I've started to think about the cooler, full of sandwiches and cold drinks, waiting for us. "Look," Samantha says, and points to a modern house that sits very close to an eroding sand dune. We can see right through its windows to the front room. All the furniture is white. "Why would they build it so close to the water?" she asks. "Aren't they afraid it's going to fall in?"

"When they built it, there was probably a lot more sand," I tell her. "But you're right. It's in a precarious spot now."

"What's 'precarious'?"

"Not very secure—or at risk. You know what that means?"

But she's no longer paying attention. Behind us, a boy and his father are launching a kite. We watch as the wind takes it, lifting it higher and higher.

"I'm getting kind of hungry," I say. "How about you?"

"Not really." She shrugs. Her hair is springing free of its unruly ponytail; red tangles and corkscrew curls whip about in the breeze. A pair of green goggles dangle from her tiny neck. She's thoroughly coated in sunscreen and sand.

"Let's head back, anyway," I say. I reach out to hold her small white hand; she lets me take it for a moment before yanking it free to run off in the wrong direction.

"Nyah! Nyah!" she calls. I refuse to chase her and stand there waiting until finally she meanders back in my general direction, refusing to acknowledge me. Though I know it's ridiculous, it hurts my feelings. We ignore one another all the way back to the blanket.

"Kids are always testing you, to see what they can get away with," Maeve says later. Her hair is wet and slicked back. She's been in and out of the water all day. Samantha is digging a hole in the sand with a plastic shovel. Alan and Justin are playing paddleball at the shoreline.

We stay until the sun is going down and the beach is emptying of sunbathers, their bright blankets and towels, umbrellas and coolers. Our skin feels salty and sunburned, and we're tired in a good way. The day reminds me of other days, other beaches, other summers. Everything is bathed in a golden light as we traipse over the white sand, like a caravan to the parking lot.

Eighty-three

On Saturday night after a dinner of hot dogs and lobster rolls in Sag Harbor, we take the ferry over to Shelter Island to see the Fourth of July fireworks. We set our blanket in the sand, shoulder to shoulder with all the others on the beach, and it occurs to me the world is becoming so crowded that one day having a solitary experience will be the greatest of luxuries.

When the fireworks begin, Samantha crawls onto her mother's lap and Alan reaches for Justin. I recall being a kid with my own family at Eisenhower Park, feeling small, my father's arms around me as the explosions reverberated in my belly.

Above us, the fireworks are so close they seem to take up the whole sky: bright snowflakes, flickering chrysanthemums, rockets, sparkly cascades, and once a flag that dissolves even as it forms.

"Ooooooo," Samantha says.

"Ahhhhh," says Justin.

We smell the gunpowder as bits of glowing ash float down. When it seems the finale is about to start, we gather our things, hoping to beat the crowd to the parking lot. The children and I watch the last explosions through the rear window of their parents' Passat, on the dark road back to the ferry. I'm seated between them and feel like a child myself, but also like a mother must feel, tired, sandy, children reaching for an arm or shoulder to lean against.

Eighty-four

After everyone has gone to bed, I find the stiff black composition book that I purchased earlier in the day and open it to its first lined page. Before personal computers, I kept journals, or diaries, in notebooks like it. I have stacks of them in storage somewhere. These days, I rarely write longhand. Who does? I use my laptop for everything. But my hope is that by doing it now, my memory will be jogged; events that seem lost will reappear. Once my pen begins to move on the page, it will all come back to me.

As quietly as I can, I make my way to the kitchen, at the back of the house. The kids are asleep across the hall. It's good to be in a house full of sleeping people, cozy and safe.

I fill a teakettle with water, turn up the flame beneath it, choose the largest mug I can find and a strong black Irish tea. I stand over the kettle and wait, afraid of its piercing whistle. At the first wisp of steam, I remove it from the burner and pour the hot water. The scent of the tea is lovely. I find myself humming very quietly.

Time feels generous. It seems to stretch ahead for hours. Carefully, I carry the tea back to the little room where I'm staying. There's a child's desk in the corner. On it sits the composition book, open and waiting. If I describe you well enough, will you come to live inside my words the way a soul occupies a body?

Holding the mug in two hands, I blow on it and take a sip. Then I place it down beside me on the desk and begin to write.

By morning, my hand is aching and I feel possessed by a kind of exhausted joy. In the east there's a pink edge to the sky. I stand and stretch my arms over my head, pull the stiff sheet back on the single bed, and lie down to close my eyes.

Eighty-five

The group is a little more ragtag than it was seventeen years ago when we were last together to record *Room Inside.* JC is living with his drum kit in a basement practice room. Dave teaches music at a high school in Pittsburgh. Alan and Fish both have working wives and young children, so it was hard for them to get away. We're still getting drum sounds when Kid shows up, trumpet in hand. He's wearing a jaunty cap. "Anybody got any weed?" he asks, half jokingly.

Drugs and alcohol have taken a toll; a couple of us are sober. We talk about the ones we knew who have overdosed, or drowned, or died of other things. Musicians don't fare well over the long haul, but remarkably, we've all made it this far. And everyone is still doing it—still playing music, undeterred by poverty, family life, career ups and downs.

When Marianne Mercurio comes through the door with her cello and her black motorcycle cap, I have to sit down. No one else has her laugh like a dolphin's cry. She's living in Woodstock now. Her long silky hair is gray and rough at the edges.

Some of the cues I've written are easily identified by my friends. Pieces of melody, hooks and bridges, from the songs of *Room Inside*. When we finally get to the redo of "Still True," we're warmed up, and it's satisfying to play the song from start to finish. We get four or five takes of it, back-to-back. I'm in the vocal booth, isolated from the rest of the band, but can see them through the little window. It feels like I'm singing the song to them.

> *Baby, all I've ever looked for is a safe place,*
> *All I've ever longed for is your warm embrace,*
> *All I've ever wanted is you.*
> *Take a good look and you'll know,*
> *It's still true*

I sing it better now than I did when I was young. I have a bit more vibrato, and my tone is warmer. It's true of everyone,

I think. A lifetime of doing one thing makes you good at it, and all of us together are a rocking, breathing, back-and-forth machine.

We order food in and listen to the playback, talk and laugh, so our bellies hurt. I remember a time backstage with Marianne and Alan at a club in Baltimore, or Philly, or some other city. They were pretending to be sumo wrestlers, walking around in a crouch, yelling in fake Japanese. Until they fell over, laughing so hard they were crying.

So many good times. What a shock it is to realize we were living in a *time,* like "after the war" or "during the Depression." It had just been *now* to us. It felt like everyone, and everything, would always be like that.

"When are you playing out?" Kid asks me, and I tell him I haven't played a show since Monday nights at Luna Park. "Why not?" he wants to know, and they all listen while I explain it.

I'm too old. I've done it too many times already, earned my place with the club owners, booking agents, record companies, and the press. It's a never-ending battle. I don't have it in me to do it again. It's all true but sounds like a bunch of excuses.

"You've still got fans out there," Kid says, and I feel that shift in perspective, a reminder that I haven't wasted my life, as I sometimes thought. I'd made something beautiful.

Eighty-six

The house my mother lives in is not the house where I grew up. I can barely recall the earlier house, though I spent eighteen years in it. Twenty-five years have passed since that house was sold and my parents moved into their "new" house. Now my mother lives alone there. I know the day will come when the house will be empty, but I can't begin to imagine it. Sometimes it hits me that I'll never see my father's face again. But I know losing my mother will be worse.

Walking briskly, it takes ten minutes to reach her house from the train. I like this town, more village than suburb. It's full of mature trees and expensive landscaping. I pass a number of massive stone churches. My mother's white split-level with black shutters is the most modest house on an avenue of impressive colonials with screened-in porches and deep green lawns. From the corner I can see my sister's SUV already parked in the driveway. My mother has turned seventy-six, and we're gathering to celebrate her birthday, just the family. It's the first year she is older than my father lived to be.

My sister's kids are home from college but have summer jobs. Josh is a busboy at an Italian restaurant, and Mack is working as a caddy at his father's club. They're supposed to drive down from Greenwich together, late in the day. I've lived out of town for half their lives and have missed a lot of birthdays and graduations. When they were small, my sister used to take them to see me play at Tower Records or Borders Books. I doubt they'd even remember it, but at the time, those performances had gone a long way toward winning their affections.

My brother-in-law, Stephen, has his nose in his BlackBerry as I come through the door. He's an attorney whose hours are never ending. He looks up and waves a greeting.

I walk past him to find my mother and sister sitting outside on the back deck. It's shaded by tall trees. I can hear children laughing and playing in the yard next door.

"I'm never letting you go back to California," my mother says as I hug her.

I lean in to give my sister a kiss. She's an attractive woman with my father's dewy eyes. "How was the train?" she asks.

"Fine," I answer, though it's well known in my family that I dislike the Long Island Railroad and try my best to avoid it.

I settle into one of the sixties lawn chairs that are almost as old as my sister and I. We have a view of the kids next door jumping into their pool. We hear their squeals before the splash. "Someone's going to fall and crack their head open," says Lynn.

"I hope not," my mother says.

As I watch them, I can easily see it happen. One of the small blond girls will hit her head and sink to the bottom of the pool. I can be over there in three seconds, I think. I see myself diving to the bottom to rescue her. I'd place her small body on the cool concrete and breathe life back into it, press down on her lungs until she coughed up pool water and opened her eyes.

But no one hits her head, or falls, or requires rescuing. They play and swim until their mother comes out. She waves to us and wraps the girls in flowery pink towels. They follow her inside, chirping like birds.

Later, we're seated around the kitchen table when the phone rings. My mother quickly hands the receiver to my brother-in-law. The boys have been in an accident, she says. I hold my breath, sure that my earlier fear, about the neighbor girls, has been a premonition. But though the car was totaled, Josh and Mack have walked away without a scratch. Thank God, we say.

My sister and brother in-law leave immediately to retrieve the boys from the Bronx hospital where they've been taken. My mother and I sit outside on the front steps and wait. We watch the cars going by, a couple of dog walkers across the street. It's nice to sit with her in the dark. I look for fireflies, but there aren't any.

"How are you, really, honey?" she asks.

"I'm fine, Mom," I say. "I'm thinking of coming back to New York, selling the house."

"Oh, you know I'd hate that," she says, lightly sarcastic, meaning the opposite.

When Lynn, Stephen, and the boys return, we sing and blow out candles and make wishes. My mother carefully tears the wrapping paper from her presents. We watch two grown boys, miraculously unharmed, wash their birthday cake down with cold glasses of milk.

Eighty-seven

As I listen to the music, my head centered between two monitors, Alan's closet-size studio seems to expand past its walls. We're layering guitar figures with transparent noise. Alan's got a bunch of guitar pedals he's trying. How to describe the thing music does? It's like drugs without drugs, God without religion, happiness for no reason. We laugh when something sounds beautiful, or loud, or silly, or wrong. We laugh until it's just right, and then we get quiet.

After we finish for the day, I ask Alan to come downtown with me. I'm in the mood to listen to songs that have just been written. He says he can't because he and Maeve have plans. I let him off the hook because I know he has no patience for most singer-songwriters, especially not the ones who go on and on.

A whole scene has sprung up on the Lower East Side during the years I've been away. There's a new generation of singer-songwriters, open mics, and hourly time slots at half a dozen clubs on Ludlow, Orchard, and Allen streets. I'm prepared to go by myself when I think of calling JC. I haven't spent any time with him in years, but once he'd sort of been my boyfriend. It had been good to see him again at the recording session.

I agree to meet him downtown at his practice room on Second Street. It's surprisingly tidy and organized, a tenement basement with carpet on the walls and floor, and black paint on the ceiling. JC's drum kit, travel cases, extra snares, and cymbals take up most of the space. "Where do you sleep?" I ask him, and he points to the spot where he drags out a rolled-up futon mattress every night. He showers at the gym, he says, and sometimes lifts free weights there, too.

"I'm used to it." He shrugs. "It's not so bad." He still looks good, although you can see the years of whiskey on him. He's heavier now and not quite as pretty. Once he was a handsome boy who used his smile to great advantage. The first time he used it on me I'd smoked all his cigarettes, though I didn't smoke. It was at an industry thing, a Christmas party. I'd been smitten on the spot.

Now I know him too well. Still it's fun to flirt, if you can call it that. He's halfheartedly trying to seduce me, and I'm laughing.

"What happened to the guy?" he asks.

"What guy?"

"The suit. Didn't you have a boyfriend? I saw a picture of the two of you in one of those rags at the grocery checkout."

"He left me for another woman." It still hurts to say it.

"No! Was he a fucking idiot?" JC rubs my shoulder.

"I guess he was."

"You're still gorgeous, you know," he says.

And I say, "*Come* on, J."

"I mean it!"

It feels good to be desired. So I let him kiss me, though we're in a basement, and I'm afraid there might be rats watching us. "Let's go hear some music," I say after the kiss.

JC shakes his head at me as if we're still kids and I'm being a tease. "Do you mind if I smoke a bowl before we go?" he asks.

"Knock yourself out," I tell him. Some things never change.

There's an open mic going on at the Rock Den, and the club is packed when we get there. We find a spot at the bar and JC orders us a couple of shots, though I'm sure he remembers I'm sober. Onstage, a dark-haired girl is singing quietly, sweetly. She cradles a Gibson hollow body in her arms. She's been raised on jazz, or influenced by singers who were raised on jazz: Billie Holiday, Nina Simone, and Jeff Buckley. Her melodies travel from major to minor and back again.

I listen as one after another singer-songwriter gets up and plays a couple of originals. Their songs recall the music of Coldplay, John Mayer, Dave Matthews, and Radiohead. Gone are the three-chord progressions and folk melodies of the seventies that influenced me and a generation after me.

A young woman with short bangs and sunglasses approaches and asks if I am who she thinks I am, and I say yes. It occurs to me that she's probably about the age you would have been, Minnow.

"Oh, play something! Will you play something? I'm a huge fan," she says.

The vibe is very low-key in the room, and I do feel like playing. I'm given a guitar and find myself seated in the spotlight, being watched intently. I'm not famous-famous, but I'm a little famous, and though most of them are too young to know who I am, just hearing that I've made records and have had a career makes me someone worth listening to.

How many thousands of times have I been in this particular position? Tuning a guitar while an audience watches and waits. Hearing my own clear voice find its way into the air. It's a good voice, I know, not strong but emotional and pure. It's always touched people in a way that surprised me.

Eighty-eight

"You never wanted children," Jules says.

We're on the phone, in the middle of another late-night conversation.

"Hrmm," I say. I've been reading to her from the black composition notebook. I write in it every day.

"We felt we needed to be alone to be artists," she says. "That we had to be selfish in order to get any work done. We thought they were little monsters who invaded our favorite restaurants and disrupted civilized conversation."

"But those were other people's children," I say. I do remember thinking that having children was what other people did when they ran out of ideas, but I can't recall when I started to feel that way, or why. There are so many layers to what's true. It seems impossible to untangle it, or get to the bottom of it.

"You're only questioning this now because it's too late to do anything about it," Jules says.

Maybe she's right. But it doesn't feel that way.

Minnow, in home movies, I'm a little girl rocking a doll.

Over and over again, I find myself wishing it were possible to be your mother, to be twenty-three or twenty-four again, walking with Gabriel on Columbus Avenue, to say to him, *"Gabriel, escúchame, por favor.* There will never be a better time. I will never love another man this way. And no one will ever take the place of our child."

Eighty-nine

For years, Alan lived alone in a dingy studio apartment, surfed the Internet, and played his guitar all day, but then he found Maeve. It seems to me he was dangling off a cliff side until she pulled him up over the edge. He's become more himself, really blossomed, as a husband and father.

I follow him through their apartment, down the hallway; it looks so lived in, so homey; children's drawings on the back of bedroom doors, toys, miniature furniture, scribbled notes, piles of laundry, everywhere evidence of love and family.

In the back room that is his studio, I say, "Get ready. You know she's going to hate it." Marta Lightman is due to arrive any moment and I expect her to give me a hard time about the score. It's always difficult for someone to appreciate the new when they've gotten accustomed to the old. The trick is to get her to give it a chance.

"She's going to love it, because it's fucking great," Alan says.

But Marta is very quiet as we take her through the key scenes. The score is spare with long minutes of silence. The songs she knows have been replaced with a single note of upright bass, a mournful bowed cello, or three black piano keys, gently played. Hammond organ breathes and sighs while a lone guitar figure repeats, its last note a question and then a resolve.

Does she think it's too slow, too spare? I'm already defending it to her in my mind when Alan cues up the birthday party scene at the end of the movie. Ashley, her mother, and other relatives are gathered around the baby as the intro to "Still True" begins. "Oh," Marta says, and moves up a little closer.

The baby's face is covered in cake and icing. It's all over her hands and her dress. "Oh, *Lisa,*" Marta says.

Alan looks at me, as if to say, *I told you so.* We let it play all the way through. The song runs long but will extend over the credits once the film is completed.

As the last note rings, I see her beaming at me. "I *love* it. It's *beauuutiful!* You guys did *so good!*"

We take a taxi to the East Side to celebrate. There's a Mexican restaurant I know of on East Ninety-eighth Street. It's very authentic, and I think Marta will like it.

She and Alan order margaritas in frosty glasses with salt on the rim. Their drinks look good, but I'm all right with my ice-cold Coke. Our waiter mixes up a bowl of spicy guacamole at the table.

"To the new score!" Marta says.

"The score!" says Alan.

"To your beautiful movie," I say. "Thank you for allowing us to be a part of it."

Ninety

There's no red carpet for *I Gave My Love,* though the screening room in Tribeca looks like a red velvet jewel box. Ashley

and her mother are supposed to be coming down from El-
lenville for the premiere. I've invited all the musicians who
played on the score. Next, the film is headed for the festivals.

Alan can't make the screening but will meet me later. We
plan to stop by the after-party for a few minutes before leaving
to pick up Maeve and the kids. It's the last weekend they have
the rental house this summer, and I've been invited to join
them at the beach.

Most of the hundred or so seats are taken as the curtain
parts in the small theater. I can see Ashley's blond head a
few rows in front of mine. She's holding Lorelei in her lap and
keeps getting up to quiet the little girl. After the third time,
I follow her into the hallway. "Let me take her, Ashley," I say.
"Go enjoy the rest of the film."

"Are you sure?" We've only met briefly, but she doesn't
seem concerned, only relieved to hand Lorelei off to me.

"Yes. I've seen it a million times."

The baby from the movie is about two and a half now. She's
got blond curls and sweet pointy ears. I give her my key chain
to play with. She holds it in both chubby hands and looks up
at me with wide blue eyes. She has that spark you hope for in
a child. A part of me imagines stealing away with her, out the
back door. But of course it's only a fleeting thought.

From the hallway, I can hear the other Ashley, the one up
on the screen, saying, "It's only now that can't be any different; the past can be anything you want!" It's my favorite line
in the movie. She's defending some half-truth on a job applica-
tion, but it means something very different to me.

At the after-party, I see JC coming toward me, glass in
hand. "Notice anything new?" he asks.

He's wearing his usual black jeans, the leather jacket. "No,"
I say. "What?"

"I'm drinking club soda!"

"Well, good for you," I say. I don't know why it's so hard for me to take him seriously.

"I've been going to meetings," he says. "I was thinking maybe we can go to one together sometime."

"I'd love that," I say, "but I'm heading back to L.A. next week, so it will have to wait for next time."

"Already?! Listen," he says, and leans a little closer. He smiles that great smile. "I've been thinking . . . We should get together sometime—you know, for real. I don't know why we never have."

I don't bother to remind him that we did get together, a long time ago. "It's too late for that, J," I say, aiming for a lightness in tone.

"What are you talkin' about? We're not dead yet!" He takes my shoulders in his hands and gives me a little shake. He's still pretty sexy. "But no one's getting any younger," he says, and kisses me on the side of the mouth. "Maybe I'll have to come out there and change your mind."

Though we both know how unlikely that is.

Ninety-one

On the East End, rain has moved in by morning. Maeve is trying to figure out something we can do to keep the kids occupied. There's a children's museum on Sagg Road, and after breakfast we all get in the car and take a ride over there. It's a pretty cool place with all kinds of activities for the kids.

Samantha and Justin are playing in an impressive spaceship facsimile when I see Sofia across the room.

An actress with personality and style, Sofia was once one of my best friends at the Café Miriam. I remember we used to sing this song together, passing through the kitchen, plates balanced on our arms: "Woman." It was from John Lennon's *Double Fantasy* album. The record was huge in 1981. John Lennon had been killed the year before. We knew every song on it.

Sofia looks the same almost thirty years later. Shag haircut and long slim legs. "Oh my God! *Hiiii!*" she says, when I come up behind her.

She still has the big, joyful personality, and it's good to find her that way. A lot of people I know have had the joy kicked out them by life. She's living in East Hampton, she says, directing plays for a local theater group. She's been divorced for ten years and has a boyfriend. Her children are grown.

"What are you doing at the children's museum?" I ask her.

She points out a boy who looks to be about three, playing alongside Justin and Samantha on the spaceship. "Can you believe it?" Sofia asks. "I'm a grandma!"

I can't believe it.

"Are you still singing?" she asks. "I have your music on my iPod. I'm so proud of you!"

I tell her I'm not singing so much, but that I'm still doing music. I don't say that I would trade it, in a second, to have what she has.

By then, Samantha and Justin are getting restless and Maeve is talking about finding a movie for them to see, so Sofia and I say our good-byes. I take her number, and she takes mine. "Let's stay in touch, honey," she says.

"Absolutely," I tell her, and hope that we will.

Ninety-two

While Maeve takes the kids to a matinee in Sag Harbor, Alan and I hang out on the porch with Lola the beagle and the paper. Maybe it's because of the rain, but I can smell fall coming. The hydrangea bush in the yard is still full of purple blossoms, and the lawn is lush and green, but soon it will be September and everything will start to change. A few Indian summer days, and the leaves turn yellow. Before you know it, it's winter again.

"You having a nice weekend," Alan asks, "in spite of the crappy weather?"

"Totally," I say. "I *like* the rain—especially out here. I wish I didn't ever have to leave." I'm feeling nervous about returning to sunny L.A. I know it's just a matter of time before I run into E and have to pretend to be over it. I feel the tears start to burn my eyes and the back of my throat.

"You *will* meet someone else, you know," Alan says. "Your life isn't over."

That's when I lose it. Kindness always does me in. I probably will meet someone, at some point. But I'll never be young again. I'll never have a child. That part is over.

"Heyyy," he says, placing his arm across my shoulder. "Don't cry." He's wearing a wool sweater that smells like wet dog. I think Lola's been rolling in it.

"You stink," I say through tears.

"Oh, thank you. Thank you very much," he says, and soon we're both laughing.

He hands me the Book Review and I pass him the Arts section. We go back to reading the paper. Lola is whining softly, dreaming. I think she's chasing squirrels in her sleep. Beyond her, I notice droplets of rain clinging to the tips of hydrangea petals.

By the time Maeve and the kids get back, the sky has cleared and the rain has stopped. "What are we doing for dinner, guys?" she calls, gently reprimanding us. We haven't done a thing about it yet.

"I'm getting the barbecue started right now," Alan says, getting up, while I follow Maeve into the kitchen.

Ninety-three

Hours later, I'm hunched over the child's desk in my room when Samantha comes in to say good night. She shows me her freshly brushed teeth and leans into me.

"Very nice," I say about her teeth.

She's wearing pajamas with ballerinas on them that are too small for her. She has such delicate wrists and ankles. "Are you still writing your story?" she asks.

"I am," I tell her. The original black composition book has become two over the course of the summer. I'm rewriting my own memories. *The past can be anything you want.*

"I'm writing a story, too," Samantha says. "It's about a girl detective. Maybe you can read it tomorrow."

"I'd love to."

"Will you read me yours?"

I look through the notebooks for something that might be appropriate to read to her and settle on the pages about fish and guinea pigs and cats. She listens with her chin in her hands.

"What do you think?" I ask when I've finished. I close the notebook.

"It's good," she says with great authority.

Ninety-four

When we get back to town on Sunday night, I find JC waiting on the front steps of the brownstone. I'm not completely surprised to see him because of his text message:

what time u comin home?

"Hey, you," he calls. His dark hair is falling into his eyes. He flips it away and reaches for me.

"Wait a sec," I say. We watch as Alan and Maeve's car turns the corner. I don't want them to see him kiss me.

I open the door and hold it for him. He follows me up the three flights of stairs to the narrow floor-through. We kiss in the dark, in the foyer, under the archway. As we move toward the bedroom I'm trying not to worry about my fifty-two-year-old body. The last time JC saw me naked I was relatively perfect. Now, under my shirt and jeans, I have cellulite, fat on my belly, and sagging breasts. Of course, he isn't young anymore either.

One day you'll be sixty, I silently scold myself, and then seventy, and eighty, if you live that long. You're going to look back on this night and know what a silly thing it was to worry about.

"Relax," he says.

Still, I don't let him take my clothes off until we're safely hidden beneath the covers.

Ninety-five

A couple of days later, I'm three thousand miles away, pulling into the driveway of my house, a 1920s bungalow at the top of a climbing street. There's a green shutter hanging off a window. The yard is dusty and overgrown. "You poor thing," I say.

I bring my bag inside, turn on the sprinklers to give the garden a drink, and then head out to my studio, a small building behind the house that used to be a garage. There are cobwebs in the corners and the guitars are covered in dust, but it's a good room with an A-line roof and a couple of skylights. It always smells a little of sawdust. I know I'll miss it if and when the house is sold.

I pull the cover off the piano and sit down to change the strings on my Martin. It's my favorite songwriting guitar and has been for as long as I can remember. Ever since Jules lent me the money to buy it. Its rosewood body has a worn patina only love and time could give it.

It's already dusk when I lock up the studio and come back inside. I turn on the TV and all the lights, but the house feels too quiet. There's no food in the kitchen except for some stale cereal. I stand at the counter and eat it straight from the box. From my window, I can see the downtown skyline glittering in the distance.

When I call Jules, she screams, "You're back!" She launches right into her news, excited to tell me about a new collector. He's interested in one of her larger mixed-media pieces. Its sale will pay the bills for months.

"You hungry?" I ask her.

"Not very," she says. "But come get me."

She's waiting out front when I pull up in my beat-up Land Rover. Her place isn't much more than a concrete box, but it looks good. She's filled the front yard with wild lilacs, hollyhocks, and black-eyed Susan.

She climbs into the seat beside me and we drive over to the health food restaurant on the Third Street Promenade, where we always go. I get the same thing every time: a veggie burger with sweet potato fries. She takes pride in her healthy diet of tofu and kale and anything with flaxseed oil. Meanwhile, she's ducking outside every fifteen minutes for a smoke.

We talk and talk, dissect every feeling and thought. It's good to get her perspective on things. She's able to place our failures and regrets in the context of archetypes and mythological tales. By the end of the night, she's convinced me that what I really need is a dog.

Ninety-six

The next morning, I begin my search, scrolling through pictures on Petmatch.com the way some look for love on a dating site. When I see her profile, I know she's the one. A border collie mix, supposedly part Eskimo dog, she's white with light brown patches. There's something tender yet intelligent in her expression. Excited, I forward the link to Jules. *Check out her name,* I write.

Like the Van Morrison song—is it kismet? she writes back. *She has a lovely face.*

We take a ride to the Valley to pick her up. I've already faxed my paperwork. I've got four hundred in cash in my pocket. Jules brings Madeline along, one of her own dogs, a half-blind Chihuahua mix who's going on twenty. "Madeline's a good judge of character," she says.

My dog has been rescued from a kill shelter and is being fostered by a couple in Reseda. They think she looks to be about a year old.

We get on the 101. It's a long drive up through the Cahuenga Pass. "Remember when Bighead called me, thinking he had called you?" Jules never tires of talking about the man who brought us together. We've had a version of this conversation more times than I can count.

"Of course I remember," I say.

"He was incredulous! 'You've got a roommate *and a dog* in that place?' I didn't know what he was talking about." Her laugh is still a girlish bell.

"I think my apartment must have once been someone's sewing room," I say. "It was teeny-tiny."

"You couldn't turn around in there! You used to bathe with your dishes in the bathtub."

"There was no kitchen sink. There was no *kitchen!*"

"I lived with Katherine. At the Normandy. Remember? We called it the Dorm-andy. And George, of course, that handsome boy. He was still a puppy."

Cigarette smoke curls up over our heads. I ask her to crack the window. Nobody smokes anymore. "When are you going to quit those?" I ask, not bothering to hide my annoyance. "You look like Popeye the Sailor!"

She laughs at that. "You know, nicotine is actually very good for cognitive function."

I roll my eyes at her. "I really do want you to quit!" I say. "I'm not kidding."

"All right, *all right,*" she says, taking a final drag before dropping the cigarette out the window. "Take it easy." She gives my shoulder a pat.

When we get to Reseda, we circle around awhile before finding the street. Some of the houses in the neighborhood have forlorn guard dogs behind chain-link fences and broken-down cars in the yard.

"There it is," Jules says. We pull up to a small ranch near the corner and lock up the car.

When my dog appears at the door, she looks like a princess in the wrong part of town. The woman fostering her holds her by the collar. "Do you still like her?" she asks.

Is she kidding? Does she think I could look at that face and change my mind? "I certainly do," I say, kneeling down to scratch her head. I haven't had a dog since I was a kid. She pants a little and raises her ears. She has dark markings across her nose, like freckles. Her eyes are soulful and bright. "What a good girl you are," I say, stroking her back. I dig into my pocket for the wad of cash and hand it to the foster woman. She counts it and grins. She has a gold crown in the place of an eyetooth.

"Okay," she says, handing the leash to me. "You go with your new mommy now, Brown-Eyed Girl."

Ninety-seven

Though I put the bungalow on the market only weeks after returning to Los Angeles, 2010 was not a good year to sell a house in need of repair, so I continue to live in Silver Lake. This morning, like most days, I carry my coffee out to the studio, Girl at my heels. I turn on my gear and stare at the first line of a song I've been stuck on all week.

If love isn't love/What do I do now?

Late in the day, Alan calls. "How's it going?" he asks. "We were just thinking about you."

It's evening there. I can hear the commotion of dishes being cleared away, Maeve asking the kids about homework. Girl is sitting at my feet, looking straight up into my eyes. I cup her head with the palm of my hand. "It's going well," I tell him.

"Glad to hear it," Alan says. "Hang on a minute. Someone wants to say hello."

When he puts Samantha on the phone, she asks me, "Did you finish your story yet?"

"Yes," I tell her. "I finished it. Do you know what some people call it when you finish a story, Samantha?"

"What?"

"They say you've put it to bed."

Ninety-eight

Good night, Little Fish.

Once I carried you in my belly and held you wrapped in a blanket in our garden, under a star. You were a ten-year-old girl with snow on her eyelashes and had a guinea pig named Z, whose fur was soft as a bunny's. You sang a harmony to your father's melody one miraculous night and were your grandfather's chess partner, a girl who loved prime numbers, asked questions, and fell in love.

Your heart was broken the way every heart breaks, when a

pet falls sick and dies, when someone you love doesn't love you back, when you have a dream that, for whatever reason, never comes true.

But your heart became full, the way every heart becomes full, of wonder and appreciation for life's beauty. Every spring, summer, fall, and winter, a surprise. Years of sunrises, stars and sandy beaches, books and music, skies with clouds that pass over, friendships that grow deep, laughter, and love, that most amazing gift, fleeting and miraculous as a comet.

In the original 1982, Minnow, you were a soul hovering, wherever it is that souls hover, and one day your soul passed over mine. We touched briefly, the way souls do, and though it didn't last long, it changed me, and I never forgot you.

There's no going back, but one day someone will read these words and won't know what was true from what was invented. That's what all memories are like, in time. When I'm gone, and Gabriel is gone, and everyone who knew us is gone, you will be still be in the world.

Dulce sueños, Minnow. Sweet dreams, my love. *Ya te extraño,* already I miss you.

Acknowledgments

To my friends and family, my early readers: your support and feedback helped immeasurably. Janet Rienstra, Paul Pimsler, Leslie Shipman, Ken and Cindy Carson, Meryl Kramer, Gregory Henry, Jacquie Leader, Kim Greist, Leon Ichaso, Gary Baker, Judith Ehrman-Shapiro, Dawn Dover, Edith Carson, Sherri Fischer, David Wecal, thank you, and especially Lisa Walker, for your generous encouragement, for reading every version, and for sharing your experiences of pregnancy and motherhood in the eighties.

Thank you to all the beautiful children I've had the privilege to know: Alex and Michael Carson; Matthew and Brayden Fischer; Max and Adam Ehrman-Shapiro; Ben Ehrman; Elizabeth, Bibi, and Madeline French; Aiden, Beatrice, and Will from East Ninety-fourth Street; Leo at five; and most especially, the delightful and lovely Chloe Carson.

Thank you to my fellow writers at the Writing S. group. Your wisdom never fails to inspire me. Thank you, Elisabeth Robinson, for our conversations about writing and the writing life, and especially for sending Sheila Gaffney my way. Sheila, I don't know what I would have done without your insights. I'm very grateful for the afternoons we spent at my table, taking the book apart and putting it back together.

Dan Kirschen, thank you for your kind help in the day-to-day, and to all at ICM and William Morrow/HarperCollins, thank you for all you do.

To Lisa Bankoff, my amazing, smart, fun, kind agent. When I am asked how I found you, I always say it was a miracle—a cold query letter sent by e-mail, late one night, and answered thirty minutes later. Lisa, thank you for changing everything.

Last but not least, thank you, Kate Nintzel. You are a mind reader and brilliant editor. I don't know how you do that. Thank you for carving away the excess and asking the right questions, for helping to bring the heart of my story into focus and Minnow into the world. I'm forever grateful.